MURDER AT
THE NEW DAWN B & B

A Cottonwood Springs Cozy Mystery - Book 9

BY

DIANNE HARMAN

Published by: Dianne Harman
www.dianneharman.com

Interior, cover design and website by
Vivek Rajan

ISBN: 9781673186338

CONTENTS

ACKNOWLEDGMENTS

To the women who told me your stories which became the basis for this book, thank you for sharing with me.

To my readers who make every minute I spend creating stories worthwhile, thank you.

To all of the people who work so hard to create my bestselling books, thank you.

To my family, Michelle, Michael, Lamine, Noelle, Liam, and Chloe, thank you for your never-ending support and ideas for future books.

And to Tom, for always being there.

Win FREE Paperbacks every week!

Go to www.dianneharman.com/freepaperback.html and get your FREE copies of Dianne's books and favorite recipes immediately by signing up for her newsletter.

Once you've signed up for her newsletter you're eligible to win three paperbacks. One lucky winner is picked every week. Hurry before the offer ends!

PROLOGUE

Brett Stephenson was glad to finally be on his own in the forest for a little while, his wife having gone back to the B & B. After the discussion they'd just had, he needed time to calm down and be by himself. If she'd stayed, he wasn't sure what would have happened. It seemed like all she'd done since they'd come to the B & B was press his hot buttons. It was almost as if she'd planned to aggravate him. And who knows? Maybe she had.

He still didn't understand why she'd insisted they come to the B & B. It wasn't like they lived that far from Cottonwood Springs. Who took a so-called vacation that was only a couple of hours from home? But she'd seen an advertisement for the New Dawn B & B online, and she'd become obsessed with the idea of spending a weekend at the B & B.

Brett had to admit that some strong words had been said on his part about going to the B & B, and he'd probably been a bit of a jerk about it, but finally he'd relented and agreed to go. He acknowledged he was lucky to have Amanda, his wife, especially after everything he'd done.

He knew he wasn't the best husband. He found himself treating her badly, even when he knew she didn't deserve it. It was almost as if he couldn't help himself. The cruel words and hurtful remarks would leave his mouth as soon as they jumped into his mind. He'd accused her of cheating when he knew she hadn't, just so he could act like he was jealous.

Whenever Brett did that, she'd stay in the background so she wouldn't attract any attention to herself. When her self-esteem was low, she didn't make him feel like he might lose her. There were plenty of times he blatantly made her think he wasn't listening to her just to keep her in line.

Another issue he had with her was that she wasn't like the woman he'd married and sometimes his frustration at that came through. He'd yell at her, say things he knew he shouldn't, and sometimes just withdraw completely. More often than not, he found solace in his cell phone. He'd pick it up and get carried away watching videos, playing games, or whatever else he could find on it to entertain himself.

Brett knew he was shutting her out, but there were times he didn't want to even look at her. When he had his phone in his hand, it was like a silent signal for her to leave him alone. That seemed to be the only time he was able to find some peace from what he felt had become a constant battle between them. Otherwise, he was constantly on edge. He'd lost count of the number of times he'd wanted to reach out and wrap his hands around her throat and strangle her, just to make her shut up.

Amanda had been sure they could rekindle their romance on this trip, and that's why she'd wanted to take it, but he didn't feel like anything could change the way things were now. They'd be okay if she just didn't make things difficult, and anymore, that seemed to be all the time. When she was being difficult, he had to raise his voice or say something to put her in her place.

After all, he was the man in the relationship. If she expected to have children with him, she better straighten up. He was perfectly happy not having kids, but lately she'd been hounding him about it. The last thing he needed was someone else expecting even more from him.

Earlier, Amanda and Brett had decided to take a walk. It was a nice evening and one of the few ways Brett could find peace and quiet was when he was walking among the trees. Something about their strength and height had always been a haven for him. Brigid, one of the owners of the B & B, had told them that some of the wooded area behind the B & B was owned by them, and as long as they didn't go too far, they were welcome to walk around.

She'd told him to talk to Linc if he wanted more information about it, but since Brett had kind of gotten into it with Linc, he decided against it. Instead, he took Brigid's word about the nearby forest, and he and Amanda had set off on their walk.

Brett tried to do things right as they walked together in the fading light. He'd really been working on controlling his anger, because it wasn't like he wanted to ruin the entire trip. But as usual, they ended up arguing, and Amanda stormed back to the B & B in another one of her moods. He sat down next to a tree and reflected on where everything had gone so wrong.

Lately, she'd been getting them more and more frequently, and he was tired of it. He'd tried to put her in her place, but that seemed to backfire, too. Normally she'd just shut up and leave him alone, but not this time. This time she was like a dog with a bone, and she wouldn't let up. She even accused him of being an abusive husband. As soon as he'd heard that word a fire blazed inside him. How dare her accuse him of that!

He picked up a stick, broke it in half, and continued to break it over and over again until it was in tiny pieces. He threw them one by one, trying to cool his frustrations. Amanda had no idea what she was talking about. Abusive? He'd show her what abusive was.

"How dare she," he said aloud to no one. The slight breeze stirred up some of the leaves that had fallen on the ground. They rustled by his feet and swirled around the tree. "Since when did she think that's the way things work with us and that she could talk to me that way? It's obvious she's lost her mind. Might even be crazy. Someone has to be filling her head with these lies, probably someone who wants to take her away from me."

He continued to grumble aloud to himself as he stood up and began to walk a bit farther into the woods. He wasn't going deep into the trees, but he needed to walk a little more before he went back to the B & B. There was so much anger and aggression building up in his chest he realized he needed to let some of it out, but being in a place with other people around made it hard for him. He needed to be where he could say what he wanted to say to his wife, without anyone else there to interfere. Linc and Eric had already shown him that they'd interfere.

"I just want my wife to be the way she used to be," he muttered. "I'm sick of all of this attention she thinks she needs. Why is she so unhappy with our life all of a sudden? It's as if what we have isn't good enough for her anymore."

When they'd first started living together, it was wonderful. She took care of everything. She'd worked part time at the flea market in her home town. Money had been tight for her, so she'd been forced to live with her parents, but then Brett had urged her to move in with him.

She'd said yes, and it was like heaven on earth for him. His laundry was always done, meals were cooked for him, and she cleaned the house. He didn't need to worry about a thing, which was nice once he got home from work. He worked on a construction crew and it could be exhausting. It was wonderful to have someone taking care of everything at home for him.

And it had been great for quite a while. But then Amanda had gotten a new job, and she wasn't home as much. The laundry started to pile up, and dinner was always late. She also stopped doing her hair and trying to look nice. He was pretty sure she'd gained weight, but he was smart enough not to say anything about it. Brett thought she had a little more padding around her middle.

"She is getting out of line," he muttered as he continued to walk through the trees. "She thinks she can call the shots just because she's started making a little money. I don't think so. That's not how it's going to be in my house, not even close Maybe I need to have a talk with her boss."

He stopped walking, certain that he'd figured out what her problem was. It was quite simple. She was cheating on him. Someone had to be filling her head with lies. Where else would she have come up with all the crazy ideas she'd had lately? Whoever it was had probably convinced her to say all those things she'd said tonight, like telling her she could speak to him as if there was something wrong with him, and accusing him of trying to control and manipulate her.

That had to be it. They were using her and twisting things around to make him look like the bad guy. They'd probably even convinced her to give him an ultimatum. "She can't leave me," he said confidently. "I'll kill her first."

He looked up, realizing it was almost completely dark. In his frustration he hadn't noticed he'd been in the woods for a couple of hours. He sighed deeply, just as he felt a solid cold object touch the back of his head.

"What the…" Brett started to say as he turned slightly to see what it was, but he never got to finish his sentence. His attacker pulled the trigger on the pistol without a word, watching Brett drop to the ground with a thud. His body laid sprawled out on the ground. They felt a pang of guilt for a moment, but they knew they'd done the right thing. Brett was no real man at all. Especially after those four last words they'd heard him say.

I'll kill her first.

They'd hidden before they'd pulled the trigger, trying to decide if this was the right thing to do. Although they'd searched for him in anger, their humanity had made them pause. After all, Brett was a human being and didn't every person have a right to life? Holding the gun there in the darkness, they weren't sure they could do it. But then he'd said those four words and it was as if something had clicked inside them.

All their goodness seemed to take a step back and someone else had stepped forward in their place. Someone who was willing to do what it took to stop Brett. Not just stop him, but also protect Amanda. Like an alter ego that had remained hidden deep within until that very moment, as if it had known eventually it would be needed. They couldn't help it. They'd seen and heard far too much to not step in and take the needed action.

Sometimes people should mind their own business, but sometimes they needed to take a stand. That was what they were telling themselves as they tucked the gun back underneath their shirt, so it was concealed from view.

Besides, what would the law do to protect her? Give her a restraining order against Brett? How many women died every month who had those? Heck, every day? Sometimes, a person had to be willing to step up and take matters into their own hands.

Turning away, they did what they could to distance themselves from the scene, both physically and emotionally. The deed was done and anyway, there was no taking it back now. Brett Stephenson was dead, and they weren't sorry. The world simply had one less abusive man in it. No one could argue that he didn't deserve what was coming to him. Everyone would agree that this was the only solution that made any sense.

CHAPTER ONE

Brigid pulled up in front of her sister's bookstore, "Read It Again," and put her car in park. It had been a few weeks since she'd been able to have a good conversation with Fiona, and it was long overdue. Life at the New Dawn B & B which she and Linc had recently opened kept her busy, but in a good way. And with her job as an editor, helping the sheriff's department as a consultant, and everything else, she just didn't seem to have the free time she used to have.

It almost seemed as though she didn't even know what free time was anymore. Not that she was complaining and after all, some good had come out of it. Because she was always on the go, she'd lost five pounds. It didn't sound like much, but her clothes were fitting better and she had a little more energy, always a plus in her book.

She grabbed her tote bag which she'd filled with her old books, climbed out of her car, and headed for the door. As she pushed it open, the familiar sound of the chime attached to the door greeted her. She stepped inside and noticed the scent of lavender that filled the bookstore.

"Brigid," Fiona said, looking up from the book she was reading. "How's it going?"

"Good," Brigid said with a smile. "I saw on Holly's schedule for

7

the week that you planned on being here. I had a few minutes free, so I thought I'd stop by and we could catch up with each other." She looked around the store. "Where's little Aiden? Is he taking a nap in the back or something?"

"He's over at the neighbors," Fiona explained. "They have a little girl about the same age, and he likes to play with her. They invited him over this morning, so I thought I'd take a little time for myself. I can't believe how long it's been since I've been in here all by myself."

"You're taking time for yourself by working?" Brigid chuckled as she approached the register and put her tote bag with her books on the counter. It was heavy, so she was glad to be rid of it. Fiona came out from behind the counter, and they walked over to their two favorite chairs. Whenever Brigid came to visit, they'd always sit in the same two armchairs near the coffeepot and talk. It was a habit by now.

"You know me. This place isn't really like work. It's a home away from home that doesn't have dishes that need to be washed or laundry to be folded," Fiona said with a laugh.

"That I can understand," Brigid laughed. "I'm getting tired of washing the pots and pans at the B & B. I don't like to put them in the dishwasher, and sometimes Linc dirties a serious number of dishes when he cooks. It was part of our deal that he'd do the cooking, and I'd clean up after him. I'm starting to think I made a big mistake." Both sisters laughed, and Fiona had to wipe a tear from her eye.

"I'll have to look at what brand the dishwasher is we just had installed. It works great on pots and pans. Maybe you could get one for the B & B," Fiona suggested. "I think it's some sort of heavy duty one that Brandon picked out. If I remember correctly, it's similar to the one they use in the kitchen out at the ski lodge."

"Maybe," Brigid nodded. "I had grand plans of never putting the pots and pans in the dishwasher, but now I'm starting to be a bit more realistic. I'd like to have some free time on my hands, at least once in a while."

"Eh, happens to all of us," Fiona said with a wave of her hand. "You're just proving you're human after all."

"So how are things with you and Brandon since you've been so busy?" Brigid asked. It had been quite a while since she'd heard anything about the clothing company that had approached Fiona about promoting a line of her clothing designs.

Fiona laughed heartily, tossing her head back. "I think Brandon's tired of seeing my sketches every day," she chuckled. "I have to admit that ever since I was accepted by Green Butterfly, I've gone overboard."

"Green Butterfly?" Brigid asked. "Is that the name of the clothing company?"

Fiona nodded. "It is. They told me to take my time because they aren't planning on releasing any of my stuff until at least next season, but I can't help it. Ever since they said yes, it's like my mind is filled with all these great ideas, and I just have to get them out of it and onto paper.

"I've been driving myself crazy trying to get them all out. Sometimes I can't sleep because I'm afraid I'll forget what popped into my head if I don't sketch it out. The next thing I know, two hours have gone by." She sighed as she stood up from her chair. "You want a cup of coffee?"

"I'm okay, thanks anyway," Brigid said. "Are they going to release your designs this fall?" She watched as her sister opened the mini fridge and got her creamer out.

"No," Fiona said as she reached for her favorite coffee mug and refilled the cup. "They work at least one season ahead of what you might think. The fall stuff is being produced to send out now. Since I'm just getting started, they told me I could either shoot for the winter or spring collections," she said with a grin. "I have to call them next week to tell them what I've decided."

"And what have you decided?" Brigid asked. "Are you shooting for next spring so you can give yourself a little extra time to figure it all out?"

Fiona laughed loudly as she finished stirring her coffee and turned back towards her sister. "Do you even know me?" she asked. "I've already picked out the winter, and I'm almost done with the spring, too."

"Are you serious?" Brigid asked, dumbfounded. "That's amazing! How in the world did you get so much done already?"

"It helps that Brandon has been so supportive. He picked up all the slack around the house on the days I went in my little office and didn't come out. He's taking care of everything so I can concentrate on what I need to do." Fiona sat back down and crossed her legs as she leaned back in the chair.

"Sounds like you picked a keeper," Brigid said with a smile. "You did a good job."

"I did, didn't I," Fiona said proudly. "What about you and Linc? How are things going now that the B & B is open and in full swing?"

"Good," Brigid said happily. "We had our only visitors check out this morning. Then we have a day or so in between before our next ones arrive. There's a young man from Florida who's coming to visit his family and a couple that's just having a weekend away from home. They're from here in Colorado, but a bit farther west."

"How do you know all of this?" Fiona gasped. "Do they tell you their life story or something?"

"Sometimes," Brigid chuckled. "After they book their room online, I call and verify everything with them and ask if they have any special needs while they're visiting. That usually gets people to talk about why they're staying with us. I don't mind. It gives me a feel for what the people are like before they even walk through our door."

"That's kind of neat," Fiona admitted. "It might be fun to start tracking where all of your guests are from."

"Holly has," Brigid said with a grin. "She created a digital map that puts a dot where our visitors are from. She's been trying to figure out where she wants to put it on the website. Linc ordered one that he wants to put up next to the entrance for all the visitors to see. We're still searching for the right pins to put in it. We don't want to have them falling out or be too hard to see."

"I know a great office supplies site," Fiona said as she tapped her chin. "I'll look and see what they have."

"I'd appreciate it. If you see anything that might work, let me know." Brigid sighed and turned to look at the bag she'd brought in. "I brought you a bag of books."

"What do you want for them?" Fiona asked, arching her brow.

Brigid knew where this was going and couldn't help but smile. It was a little game she and her sister liked to play. "Your love and affection," Brigid smirked.

"You got it, and anything else you want to read. On the house," Fiona winked.

Brigid shook her head. She didn't know why her sister insisted on their little exchange each time, but it always made them both smile. If she was being honest with herself, Brigid would have to admit she kind of liked it. It was as if they'd found a new way to say I love you to one another.

"When can I see your creations for the clothing line?" Brigid asked, shifting the attention back to her sister.

"Come over to the house. I'll show you more than you could ever want to see," Fiona said happily.

"I will," Brigid said. "I should be able to break free once we get the new guests checked in. We're kind of doing a thorough cleaning while the place is empty, just to make sure it stays in tip-top shape. I don't want any dust bunnies moving in when I least expect them."

"Those little suckers like to just appear out of nowhere, don't they?" Fiona chuckled. "I found a whole horde of them under my china cabinet when we rearranged some furniture a week or so ago. I couldn't believe it."

"Cleaning is a job that's never done," Brigid lamented. "But it feels so good when you sit back and see the results from at least trying."

"So true, and for me, that's usually when Aiden's asleep. Once he wakes up, he takes out everything I've put away," Fiona said with a mock pout. "And he's into everything. His favorite thing is to open all the cabinets he can reach and pull everything out. I swear he thinks it's a game we play."

Brigid laughed. "I can only imagine. He seems as if he's a fairly ornery little kid."

"He comes by it honestly, that's for sure," Fiona confessed. "Between me and how Brandon was when he was little, I'm surprised Aiden's not swinging off the ceiling fans and setting the yard on fire."

"Surely Brandon wasn't that bad," Brigid said with a laugh.

"Okay, maybe not quite that extreme. But according to my mother-in-law, Brandon loved to get into absolutely everything. She said when he was two, she left him sitting in front of the TV to go make him a sandwich, and when she came back, he'd climbed to the top of a big bookshelf they had. She was amazed he hadn't hurt himself. And this was before the era of babyproofing and things like that."

Fiona's attention was caught by a flash of light caused by a car driving by outside. As she looked out the front door, she blew on her cup of coffee and took a sip.

"Well, I'm glad Aiden hasn't done anything like that, yet," Brigid sighed. "I think that would give me a heart attack."

"Me, too," Fiona said as she turned back to her sister. "I can't imagine what went through my mother-in-law's mind when she saw him up there like that."

"Probably nothing but getting him down," Brigid said. "At least you know your son comes from a line of acrobats," she joked, trying to make light of the situation. She understood why her sister would be concerned though. That would be terrifying.

"No kidding," Fiona said as she shook her head. "I wonder if I should just wrap him in bubble wrap. He's constantly trying to walk under the dining room table and not realizing that he's got to duck to get under it. Sometimes he just barely catches it with his little head." She shook her head. "I think it makes him mad more than anything. But he screams like a banshee every time."

"Aww, I bet that smarts," Brigid said. "Poor little guy. It's tough getting bigger and finding out you can't do the same stuff you once could. And before long, he'll be Holly's age."

"Don't remind me," Fiona said softly.

"It might seem terrifying, but I have to say, I don't see why people are always complaining about teenagers," Brigid shrugged.

"That's because you managed to get a good one," Fiona pointed out. "I know one woman whose stepdaughter used to try to convince everyone she was abused when she was only being punished. She told everyone that her stepmother took stuff away to be mean, when in reality, the girl was being a jerk around the house and refused to do anything besides eat and watch TV."

"That's horrible," Brigid gasped. "Why would she do something like that?"

"Who knows?" Fiona shrugged. "The point is, just because you have a good one doesn't mean they all are."

Brigid nodded, willing to accept that she just might have gotten lucky with Holly.

CHAPTER TWO

Amanda Stephenson had always done everything she could for her husband. From the moment they met, she'd loved him with every fiber of her being. She always tried to anticipate his needs and do things before he'd even ask. Her love had always been a deep well, but lately she'd begun to wonder if that love might be starting to dry up. It was as if she'd given him all the love she could muster and he'd bled her dry.

She was beginning to feel as though things were slipping away between the two of them. The peaceful and happy moments were few and far between. She was aware that a lot of it could be her fault, because she'd gotten tired of bending over backwards for someone who wouldn't do the same for her.

When she'd first met Brett, Amanda had worked at the local flea market. She'd had limited hours there and because of that, had moved back in with her parents, which had worked out well, because her mother had gotten sick around the same time. It wasn't life-threatening, but her mobility had suffered.

Her mother hadn't taken to being cared for very well, and it had been a toll on her father who struggled to be a caregiver. After her mother had her surgery and seemed to be on an upward trend, she and Brett decided to live together before they got married. They'd been dating for a while by then and were completely inseparable.

When he asked her if she'd consider it, she leaped at the chance. Everything seemed to work out so well.

But a few weeks before she moved in with him, he'd started to change. Brett would get jealous if he came to visit her at work and saw a man at the register talking to her. He even admitted once that he didn't like seeing her talking to other guys, because it made him feel angry. At the time, Amanda had thought it was cute when he got upset when she spoke to other men.

She thought it meant he cared for her and wanted to protect her. That he was worried she'd find someone else or something silly like that. She'd dismissed it as him just being overly protective and as a sign that he truly cared for her. What girl didn't want a man who was willing to defend her honor? But her mom had seen the warning signs and once she'd said something to her daughter, when it was just the two of them.

"No man should want to lock you up in a tower all for himself. He should be so proud of you he'd want to take you out and show you to the world. What good is a beautiful flower that's kept inside? The most beautiful flowers always bloom best when they're out in the sun," her mother had told her a few days before she'd moved in with Brett.

"But Mom," Amanda had argued. "He loves me. He just wants to make sure nobody hurts me." They'd been sitting together on the porch, enjoying the morning air, when the conversation took place. Thinking back, Amanda remembered it well and the look of concern that was on her mother's face.

"Is that what he's doing?" she'd asked. "It sounds more like someone trying to tell you who you can and can't talk to."

Amanda realized now that she probably should have paid more attention to her mother's warnings. But soon after that she'd quit her job. Brett had said she could just relax and take care of their home, along with planning their small wedding, instead of worrying about a job. At the time, Amanda had thought it was a dream come true. She could catch up on her reading list and plan their quaint little wedding.

Every day she'd done all the housework and dinner was ready for him when he came home. She was always doing whatever she could to make sure Brett was happy. Looking back, she knew he'd never told her she had to do those things. It had been her choice. But eventually, it was as if he expected it all the time. He'd get angry when she didn't get something done or she was too tired. She'd started sleeping more and more, not taking care of herself or caring about things like she used to.

That was when she'd gone to the local factory that made diplomas and gotten a full-time job. It was shortly after her mother had died that she'd made the decision to apply. She'd been lying in bed and had drifted off when she dreamed of her mother. She'd insisted that Amanda get her life back on track and not let Brett hold all the money. She deserved to have some of her own. The company called her two days later for an interview, and they'd hired her immediately.

Getting a full-time job gave her the confidence she'd been lacking. It also didn't hurt that she was starting to make friends again. She had the ability to get out from under his thumb, and it made life easier. The fact that he couldn't just waltz in and see who she was talking to at any given moment had given her a sense of safety she hadn't realized she'd been missing.

Amanda brought her attention back to the present and what she was doing. They'd be heading to Cottonwood Springs soon to spend the weekend, and hopefully, get a little recharge for their sagging marriage. She wanted to tell Brett how she felt while they were away and with some luck, he'd see what was right in front of his face - that he was a lucky man who had a doting wife.

He didn't need to get angry with her all the time. Amanda might not be waiting on him hand and foot now, but that was how life really was. There was supposed to be some sort of give and take in marriage, not just all give on her part and all take on his. She needed a partner, and she hoped that being in a different setting and having a real conversation about how she felt would make him open his eyes and recognize the problem.

As she folded her clothes and put them in a small overnight suitcase, she sighed as she looked around their bedroom. Her thoughts flashed back to the argument they'd had the night before and she shuddered. Brett had gotten really angry when it was seven o'clock and his dinner wasn't ready. He'd yelled and hovered over her as she cooked, waving his hands. She'd tried to stand up for herself, but that only made him angrier, so she became quiet and just allowed him to rant.

He'd really startled her though when he'd gotten in her face. For a split second, she thought he might hit her. She smelled the beer on his breath and saw the fire in his eyes as he stood in front of her, huffing and puffing with anger. That was when she did the only thing she knew to do. She placed her hands on his chest and apologized as if she were a little girl. Making promises and telling him all the things he wanted to hear so he'd sit back down and relax, but he wouldn't.

He'd yelled one more time and then in a flash, shoved her against the counter. After that she'd just stood there crying. He'd stared at her for a moment in disbelief before storming off in silence.

She didn't know why she allowed him to make her cower. It certainly wasn't the kind of person she was raised to be. No, her mother had always taught her to speak up for herself and never back down. But now she'd lost her nerve, and she was allowing this man to bully her. She saw that and recognized it, but she wasn't sure what she could do about it.

She wasn't making enough money to put anything back into savings. Every penny she earned usually went to something the house needed or her car. But hopefully, things would change this weekend, and she wouldn't have to worry about that anymore.

This weekend, she wanted to lay all the cards on the table. She was going to hold a mirror up to him, so that he could see just how controlling and manipulative he'd become. And it wasn't all yelling either. Most of what he'd done was in small ways, like making her feel bad for stopping somewhere before coming home from work. Or not allowing her to message her friends before she asked him. Insinuating she was cheating on him when she was on social media.

It had to stop. She was a grown woman who deserved to live a life she controlled, not him. She shouldn't have to answer to him. Granted, if he wasn't so demanding, and if he asked nicely, it would be different. But he was forever using words to hurt her and that had to stop.

Amanda looked at the clock and saw that Brett would be home soon. She finished what she was doing and headed out of their bedroom and down the hall to the kitchen. She needed to start dinner, so he wouldn't yell at her as soon as he came in. She needed him to be calm.

That's why she'd gone to the store today and bought all his favorites. He was in bad mood anyway about spending money on the B & B, even though she was paying for it, so she hoped this would lighten his mood. Amanda realized she was still playing into his hands, but for the time being she had to.

A small voice in the back of her mind spoke up. *What are you going to do if he's still mad? Or worse, decides to ignore you completely?* Which was something he was known to do when he had other things he wanted to focus on. Another one of his twisted ways of thinking. It was okay for him to ignore her, but she better not do it to him.

"Then I'll make him talk to me," she said aloud to herself and then stopped. She remembered he'd installed security cameras that watched the outside of the house and had microphones. Now he could hear what was going on near those cameras anytime he logged onto the app.

Something struck a nerve with her right then. How fair was it that he could watch her, dictate who she could talk to, and what she should be doing with her time? How had things gone so terribly wrong? And what would she do if things escalated?

Shaking her head, she decided she couldn't worry about that right now. If she got herself worked up, it would show on her face when he came home and that definitely wouldn't be a good start to the evening. But even as she was thinking that, another thought pushed through.

What if he decided to hurt me? Would I defend myself or would I just let him kill me?

Amanda shuddered at the thought before turning on some soothing music on the radio and forcing those thoughts out of her mind. She couldn't think like that. He hadn't hit her, so why did her mind decide to go there? But she knew that deep down it was a fear of hers. After all, he was much bigger than she was and worked a job that was physically demanding.

He was muscular and it would definitely hurt if one day he did decide to hit her. What if all it took was one time? One solid swing, and she didn't get back up? There were stories of men who did that. Could it happen to her? He'd already pushed her. Technically that wasn't a hit, but it was still something. Especially if her hip had anything to say about it.

"Stop," Amanda said aloud to herself. She couldn't think like that. She had a plan and needed to stick with it. She had to get him to the New Dawn B & B and have a talk with him when they were alone. And if he didn't listen? Well, that just wasn't acceptable. She had to stand up for herself, whatever that looked like. And if that meant taking matters into her own hands, so be it. Brett would be put in his place after this weekend, and whatever it took, she had to do it.

There would be no going back to how things used to be. She'd make sure of that.

CHAPTER THREE

"I'm going over to Fiona's after this couple shows up and they get checked in," Brigid said as she and Linc sat on the couch at the B & B. They'd just finished making sure everything was in order for the day and were taking a short break.

Their young male visitor, Eric Newberry, had arrived yesterday, and he was off visiting his family. They lived nearby, and he'd been anxious to go see them. Kind and polite, it seemed like he'd be a great guest.

"Okay," Linc said. "I need to finish doing some yard work today. What are you going to Fiona's for?"

Brigid shifted on the couch to face Linc and tucked a wayward strand of hair behind his ear. It had gotten a little longer recently because he hadn't had time to go to the barber shop, but Brigid liked it. "She's going to show me the clothing designs she's sending the company for her line," she said distractedly. It had become a habit to play with Linc's hair now.

"I bet she's eager for you to come over so she can show them to you," he said as he turned towards her. His eyes softened as he studied her face. "I'm glad you and your sister are still so close."

"So am I," Brigid said. She'd never thought about how lucky she really was to have her sister be such a part of her life. She knew not many people stayed that close with their siblings. How many people had she known when she lived in L. A. who were estranged from their entire family? It had always made her feel sorry for them. She couldn't imagine a life like that. It had to be very lonely.

Even when she'd been living in Los Angeles, she and Fiona had still kept in touch. It hadn't been as often as they talked now, but that was simply because it was easier now. Trying to imagine what life would be like without Fiona around was almost impossible. She was such a fixture in Brigid's life it would be like taking away her favorite food. Miserable.

The sound of a car pulling up made them both turn to look out the front window. An older SUV parked and then both doors opened.

"I'd say that's probably them," Linc said. "Want me to check them in?"

"No, I can do it," Brigid said as she stood up. "You just sit and rest before you have to go out and do the yard work." She bent over and gave him a kiss before heading over to the check-in desk. She made sure the tablet was ready for her to check them in as she waited. Eventually, they pushed the door open and stepped inside.

"Good afternoon," Brigid said cheerfully. "Welcome to the New Dawn B & B."

"Thank you," the woman said. "We're glad to be here."

"Yes, yes we are," the man said. "I'm Brett Stephenson and this is my wife, Amanda." He was a tall man, around 6' 2" with short, dark blonde hair and a dark complexion, as if he spent a lot of time outside. Amanda was shorter than he was, but still relatively tall, around 5' 8". She had light brown hair that was pulled back in a ponytail. She gave Brigid a quick and gentle smile before looking away again.

"Nice to meet you," Brigid said as she began to check them in. "I see you prepaid for the weekend, so all I need to do is get you checked in and show you to your room."

"Sounds great," Brett said. "That reminds me," he turned to his wife while Brigid typed in their information. "Did you bring my pillow?"

She looked at him wide-eyed. "No, I thought you would."

Brett turned to fully face his wife. "Why would I go out of my way to get it when you said you were going to the bedroom? Obviously, I assumed you'd grab it."

Brigid watched the exchange, unsure of what was going on. It was clear that Brett was choosing his words carefully. His tone was measured, as if he really wanted to raise his voice.

"I-I'm sorry," Amanda stammered. "I really thought you were going to get it."

"Let me show you to your room," Brigid said quickly. She heard Brett exhale loudly before he turned and plastered a grin on his face. It was so forced that it hardly passed for a smile.

"Sorry about that," he said. "I'm just a little picky about my pillows. Sometimes it's hard for me to sleep if I don't have the right one."

"Not a problem," Brigid said politely as she walked around the desk. "We have a variety of pillows here for just that reason. I'm sure we can find one that will work for you."

She gestured for them to follow her down the hall as she led them to their room. She'd been struggling to find the right words to diffuse the tension in the most diplomatic way possible. No couple should start their stay with a disagreement. If she could do anything to help out, she would.

23

"I appreciate that. Thank you," Brett said as Brigid stopped outside their door. "I'm sure I'll figure something out."

"Let us know if you need anything at all. I'm leaving soon, but my husband is going to be working out in the yard, so if you need anything just look for him. We want to make sure your stay is a comfortable one, so if the pillows that are already on the bed aren't to your liking, please tell one of us. I can be fairly picky about my pillow too. Don't be shy."

She looked them both in the eye before handing over the key to their room and allowing them to let themselves in. Brett took the key and quickly pushed it into the lock.

"Thank you so much," Amanda said softly. "I'm sure we'll be just fine." When she looked Brigid in the eye, Brigid noticed the pain that was there. She was like a small child hiding behind something, too nervous to step out. Brigid wondered if they were having marital problems, but she also knew better than to assume.

Couples fought for a lot of different reasons and it could happen at any time. There was always a chance they were just struggling in their relationship right now and hoped this weekend would help set it right again. Brigid wondered if there was anything she could do. She promised herself she'd try to help them out in any way she could think of.

"Wow," Amanda said as she stepped into the room after her husband had unlocked it. "This room is gorgeous."

"Thank you," Brigid said proudly. "Enjoy yourselves," she said before turning and heading back down the hall. She heard the soft click of the latch as they shut the door to their room.

When she got back to the main room, Linc stood up and walked over to her.

"Did that guy rub you wrong, too?" he asked in words that were barely above a whisper.

"He did seem a little… aggressive," Brigid whispered back. "But we don't know what's going on with them. Maybe they had a rough trip or their relationship isn't going well right now."

"You're right," Linc conceded. "But something about him bothers me."

"Oh?" Brigid asked. "Why do you think that is?" She was working with the computer, entering that their latest guests were in their rooms.

"I'm not sure," Linc said thoughtfully. "But I think it's because he reminds me of someone I knew a long, long time ago."

"And that's bad?" Brigid asked as she finished with the computer entries.

"Yeah, it is. Considering who he's reminding me of," Linc said as he looked over his shoulder, almost as if he were keeping an eye out for Brett.

"Who does he remind you of?" Brigid prompted.

"The husband of one of my coworkers a long time ago," Linc said softly. "The guy ended up beating her almost to death one night when she decided to leave him."

"Are you serious?" Brigid gasped. "That's horrible. Why didn't she leave him sooner?"

"Just one of those situations," Linc shrugged. "She didn't think he'd ever do that. He'd been emotionally abusive and controlling for a long time. That night was the first time he'd ever laid a hand on her, but when he did…" Linc let his sentence trail off as if he didn't feel it needed to be finished.

"Well, I hope you're wrong. I'd hate to think that young lady in there was in trouble." Brigid shook her head, her heart hurting for her guest.

"I hope so, too," Linc sighed. "I really do."

Brigid let out a puff of air. "Well, it won't do us any good to sit around and speculate. The only thing we can do is watch out for any warning signs and hope we're wrong. Like I said, maybe they just had a tense ride here and need some time to rest.

"We've been snappy with each other before. Every couple has. I'd hate for anyone to assume you were abusive just because you'd had your fill of me at that moment." She leaned over and bumped him with her elbow.

"Yeah, I guess you're right," he said. "Well, you better head on over to Fiona's and see what she's been working on. I'm sure she's chomping at the bit to show you."

"Probably," Brigid chuckled. "I sent her a text earlier to let her know I'd be on the way after our guests arrived."

"I love you," Linc said as he leaned in to give her a kiss. "I'll hold down the fort while you go and enjoy yourself."

"Thank you," she said after she kissed him back. "If you need anything, just let me know."

"I doubt I'll need your help with the yard work, but thanks," he pointed out.

She squeezed his hand as he turned and walked towards the back door of the B & B, leaving her alone with her thoughts. She really hoped this couple wouldn't end up being a nightmare.

She headed back over to their house, which was located next door to the B & B. She smiled when she saw Jett laying on the porch. "You want to go visit Fiona with me?" she asked the big dog as he lifted his head. "You want to play with the baby?"

Jett stood up and began wagging his tail. Little Aiden wasn't exactly a baby anymore, more like a toddler, but he and Jett loved each other. Jett would lay down and let the boy pet him and crawl all over him. When Aiden got a little older, Brigid was sure Jett would play fetch with him. They were almost inseparable when they were together. She had the feeling that Jett felt as if he were Aiden's babysitter when the boy was around.

Jett followed her inside as she grabbed her purse and keys. "Well, I take it that's a yes," she said with a small smile. She led him back outside and he trotted along ahead of her, waiting patiently by the side of the car for her.

"If that dog was any smarter, I'd be scared," she said to herself as she walked up to him and opened the rear door of her car. He jumped into the back seat without any trouble, and she shut the door behind him. "I swear, he's like a human in a dog body," she mumbled as she opened the driver's door and climbed in.

CHAPTER FOUR

Linc had just finished his work on the mower and parked it in the shed on the edge of the property. He was hot and sweating, so he grabbed a drink from the little fridge he kept out there. It wasn't much, but it was nice to have a cool beverage handy without having to walk all the way back to the house. He reached for a rag, wiping the sweat from his forehead before leaning against the door frame to rest.

He looked out onto the lawn that he could see from the shed and smiled to himself. One of his favorite things was seeing his yard freshly mowed. He loved the smell and the way everything was so uniform. After he'd had a chance to cool down, he'd get back at it by taking care of the edges and then checking the flower beds for weeds. But for now, he was allowing himself to take pleasure in a job well done.

As he stood there, mentally basking in a job well done, he thought about how happy he was that he and Brigid had opened the B & B. Granted, it wasn't something he'd have ever dreamed of doing when he was younger. Truth be told, he always thought he'd be a professional snowboarder, make a lot of money, and then retire young.

Then he learned the lesson that fun doesn't always pay the bills. He smiled to himself. But if he had been a snowboarder, he never would have met Brigid or Holly. There was nothing on this earth that was worth losing those two.

A text alert on his phone pulled him from his thoughts.

Hey, I'm going to go to the movies with Wade after work if that's okay with you? It was Holly.

No problem, you need money? he sent back.

No, I've got it. Thanks though, Holly replied.

"That kid," he said with a smile. He couldn't even begin to articulate how he felt about her. She was so incredibly smart and funny. Everything he'd always imagined a daughter of his to be. He didn't care that she wasn't biologically his, but adopted. It made no difference to him. She was his daughter, pure and simple. He knew he'd miss her terribly when she went to college in a couple of years. Linc felt a little teary-eyed just thinking about it.

"Just leave me alone," he heard a woman say in a loud voice. She sounded frustrated, maybe even angry, but definitely upset. Linc paused, the sports drink bottle touching his lips.

"Amanda, get back here." Linc recognized that voice, it was the guy who had checked in earlier, Brett. Linc stepped back into the shed, deciding it was probably smart to stay out of it. After all, Brigid might be right. This couple could just come off as having a bad relationship for some reason he didn't know about.

Maybe they'd gotten into an argument on the way to the B & B or something like that. No couple agreed all the time, that he knew for certain. Sometime people who'd been married for a while bickered about the smallest of things. He should really just let them have their privacy. What happened in another couple's relationship wasn't his business. Who was he to judge?

"Please, just stop," Amanda pleaded. It almost sounded as if she were crying. Linc couldn't help but peek out through the crack of the door. The pleading in her voice made it impossible for him to not at least keep an eye on things. He saw her sit down on a bench near the strip of trees that divided the yard of the B & B and their house.

"Amanda, this is not the place for this," Brett growled. He sounded as though he were trying to keep his voice down, but was quickly losing his temper.

"That's why I just want you to go back inside. Let me have a little space for a moment, please," she begged as he drew closer.

Linc saw Brett stand up straighter and take the last few steps so that he was standing over her. "Amanda, if you don't get off that bench right now," he ground out. His tone may have been level sounding, but his posture was anything but. He looked as though he were squaring his shoulders for a fight, totally intimidating her. That was all Linc needed to see.

"Hey guys, how's it going?" Linc said cheerfully as he stepped out of the shed. Both Brett and Amanda looked quickly in his direction, shocked there was someone else around.

"Oh, uh, good," Brett said as he took a step back and turned towards Linc. "Sorry if we're bothering you. We're just having a bit of a disagreement."

"No bother," Linc said carefully as he looked from Brett to Amanda. He could see that Amanda was trying to hide her tear-stained face. "Can I help with anything?" he asked. He realized he probably should have looked at Brett too when he asked that question, but he couldn't bring himself to.

"We're good, thanks," Brett said dismissively. "We were just having a little talk."

Linc nodded but continued looking at Amanda. "Ma'am? Are you okay?" he asked politely when she didn't look at him. That was what he wanted, for her to make eye contact. He wanted her to see that he wasn't a man like her husband. If she needed help, he would provide it.

While still looking away, she nodded. Sniffling, she wiped her hand across her face and turned to face him. He could see she was doing her best to push it down, and he could also see that her emotions were churning just below the surface.

"I'm fine," she said softly. She managed to meet his gaze, but not for long.

"Why are you asking her that?" Brett said evenly.

"Because she doesn't look fine to me," Linc said as he turned to face Brett. The guy might have a few less years and a few more inches in height than Linc, but that didn't mean he was going to sit there and watch the man mistreat his wife. It was the right thing to do. "And I was raised to make sure that a lady always feels safe, no matter what the circumstances."

"Well, she is," Brett ground out. "Now I would appreciate it if you let us have our privacy. This doesn't concern you."

Linc held Brett's gaze for probably just a moment longer than he should have, but he wanted Brett to see that he was serious. Linc knew he was walking a thin line. Abusive men could make it so much worse on their victims if they tried to get help. But Linc couldn't allow her to think for a moment that she wasn't in a safe place. He couldn't protect her once she went home, but while she was here at his B & B, he would. If she needed help, she'd come to the right place.

Turning, Linc forced himself to shut the shed door and head towards the B & B. He'd left the weed eater near the front, and he still had plenty to do. He told himself that he'd keep an eye on Brett.

When he'd walked a bit of a distance from them, he heard them begin to speak in hushed tones. He took a deep, leveling breath and forced himself to keep walking. Amanda needed to want his help in order for him to give his help to her. It wouldn't do any good if she didn't understand that she needed his help.

But what about Rebecca? A voice in the back of his head pointed out. *She didn't know she needed help and look what happened to her. What if the same thing happens to Amanda because you didn't step in?*

Linc shook his head. He wouldn't allow himself to think that way. After all, he couldn't save everyone in the world. But the thought still continued to nag at him. He knew Brett's kind. Big brutes that think it's okay to use their fists. Pushing and pushing, harder and harder until someone ends up hurt... or dead. The only way to stop someone like that was to take matters into your own hands.

If Linc had known back then what would happen to his coworker, Rebecca, he would have stepped in. He could have handled her husband much better than Rebecca did. She'd been a sweet woman who ended up permanently scarred because of her husband.

When he got to where his weed eater was laying against the side of the B & B, Linc did his best to force the situation from his mind. For now, there was nothing else he could do. But if he saw something he didn't like, he couldn't swear he wouldn't get involved. That was just the kind of man he was. If someone needed help, he'd be darned if he wouldn't give it to them.

CHAPTER FIVE

"These are all gorgeous, Fiona," Brigid gushed as she looked over the design sketches Fiona had done. Each one was unique and colorful, just like her sister. "I absolutely love the shape of this one," she said as she pointed to a sweater with an asymmetrical neckline. It was sketched as if it were made from a heavier, knitted yarn that looked flirty, but also warm.

"Really?" Fiona asked, surprised. "I kinda figured you'd go for something more like this." She dug around in her stack of sketches and pulled one out. It was more of a traditional outfit that admittedly did look like something Brigid would wear.

"Oh, I like that one too," Brigid nodded. "But the other one is just different. All of the colors, shapes, and textures. I like it."

"Thanks," Fiona said, blushing a little. "I'm glad." She sighed and began to shuffle through the stack again, not necessarily looking for anything, just to have something to do with her fingers. "I have to admit that I'm pretty nervous about all this. So far, I haven't shown them to anyone but you and Brandon. I just hope everyone else likes them, too."

"They will," Brigid said gently. "There's no way these won't go over well with the designers. And if for some reason they don't, it won't be because of you or your designs. These people wanted to snatch you up pretty fast. If they liked what they saw, I bet you'll catch someone else's eye."

"I hope so," Fiona sighed. "I really want this."

"You'll get it. Soon, everyone will be wearing your clothes," Brigid said confidently.

"Can you imagine?" Fiona asked. "Having my designs in those big department stores at the mall?"

"I don't think you're shooting high enough, girl. I'm thinking about celebrities and internet stars. The people everyone watches to see what they're wearing, so others can be just like them. Think they're called influencers or something like that. Just you wait, give it some time and you'll be too big for this little town," Brigid said encouraging her sister to think bigger.

Why was it that even when it was obvious she was becoming successful, Fiona still couldn't see her potential?

"I don't know about that," Fiona said shaking her head. "That seems like a bit of a stretch. Besides, I don't think I'd ever want to live anywhere else. Everyone I know is here. Why would I want to give up all that?"

"It's not a stretch," Brigid insisted. "You've got it in you. Just keep trying and have faith. You'll see. One day it will all sink in. I look forward to hearing you say I was right." She gave her sister a cocky grin and then laughed. "And with as much money as you're going to make, I'm sure you'll be able to live anywhere you want."

"I don't know if I'd ever give you the satisfaction of telling you that you were right. Your head might explode," Fiona chuckled. "So what's going on with Linc and Holly?" she asked.

"Holly's over at Wade's house, and Linc is keeping an eye on the B & B. He had some yard work to do," Brigid explained. "He was trimming the bushes with the clippers when I was leaving."

"I don't know how you do it," Fiona said as she leaned back on the couch and set her sketches to the side. "Having strangers around all the time would really bother me, particularly dealing with their drama. Seems like a nightmare. I can only imagine what it must be like. It's probably awkward at the breakfast table."

"Most of the time it's not like that at all," Brigid explained. "Normally people are very kind and friendly. They don't give us any drama or anything like that. Usually breakfast is just people making polite conversation. We've had one or two who seemed to think we wanted to know their life story, but that doesn't happen very often."

"Why do I feel like there's a 'but' in there somewhere?" Fiona asked with a raised eyebrow.

"Well, we do have this couple that I'm a little worried about," Brigid said. "They haven't really done anything yet that would be considered a problem, but I'm not so sure about the husband. He seems a bit overbearing."

"Really?" Fiona said, looking surprised. "Why do you say that?"

"He just seemed overly bossy with his wife. It was like he didn't take responsibility for his own actions," Brigid explained. "She seemed to almost cower in front of him. I've never seen a man treat his wife that way. You had to have been there to fully understand what I'm talking about. It was an odd vibe, and I didn't like it."

"Maybe it was nothing," Fiona shrugged. "Every couple has bad days. I'd hate for someone to judge Brandon and me right after we've had an argument. We can be fairly cold and distant. Maybe that's how they are?"

"That's what I keep telling myself," Brigid admitted. "Besides, it's not like I can really ask the woman if her husband beats her or something. She didn't have any bruises or anything that I could see."

"Not all abuse is physical," Fiona pointed out. "Sometimes the mental abuse can almost be worse. Making women doubt their worth and treating them like they don't count. It's so disheartening." She looked down sadly. "I hope that's not the case, but you just never know."

"Maybe that's what's going on," Brigid sighed. "I feel terrible, because I keep thinking I should be doing something, but at this point, I'm really not sure what I can do."

"You can't save the world, Brigid," Fiona said sympathetically. "I know your heart's in the right place, but sometimes you really can't help people. They need to find the strength within themselves to get away from a situation. That's the reality of it."

"It just breaks my heart," Brigid admitted. "To know someone may need help and not be able to provide it."

"I know. You're a good person." Fiona reached for her sister's hand and squeezed it. "That can be a good thing most of the time, but I think right now you need to figure out how to shut it off and ignore it as much as you can. You don't want to upset them if it turns out you're wrong."

The front door opened and Brandon walked in with Aiden on his hip. "Hello, ladies," he said as he closed the door behind him. "How are you two doing on this beautiful day?"

"Hey," they both said in unison. "We're doing good. How was the park?" Fiona asked.

"Well, I think Aiden may have made a new friend," Brandon chuckled. "We took a whole bag of toys for him to play with and naturally he'd rather play with a couple of sticks he found. But there was another little boy who came over and wanted to play with him. They still played mostly with the sticks and rocks, but honestly, that's fine with me. Aiden seemed to get along well with him."

"That's so sweet," Brigid smiled. "If only everything were as simple as toddler friendships."

"Sometimes those aren't so simple," Fiona said quickly. "I don't know how many times I've seen him get irritated if someone else plays with his favorite toy."

"That's very true," Brandon agreed. "Only certain friends can play with certain things. He's got one heck of a personality on him. I wonder where he gets that from?" he said, giving Fiona a pointed look.

"What? Me?" she asked with mock surprise.

Brigid's phone began to ring as she laughed at her sister. She dug in her purse while Brandon and Fiona continued to talk to each other. When she finally pulled it out, she saw that the call was from Linc.

"It's Linc. He probably needs my help with something," she said as Fiona and Brandon paused in their conversation.

"Hey, how's the yard work going?" Brigid asked as she answered the phone.

"Okay, I guess," Linc said. "But I think we may have a situation with that couple." His voice was quiet, as if he was trying to keep from being overheard.

Brigid paused, unsure what to say. "What do you mean?"

Linc explained to her everything that had happened after he put the mower away. He told her about hearing the argument, the look on Amanda's face, and how overbearing Brett had been. "Brigid, I wanted to punch that guy," Linc said. "The way he was treating her made me so mad. I have half a mind to go back and set him straight."

"Take a couple of deep breaths," Brigid said as she tried to calm him down. "I'll come home right away. Maybe it just looks bad because we don't know what's going on with them. Sometimes our imaginations can make things seem far worse than what they really are," she reminded him.

"I'm trying. This is the first time I've been ready for a guest to leave," he confessed. "And I kind of feel badly about it. I don't want to overstep my boundaries, yet this guy just sets off every warning bell of mine."

"Don't do anything drastic, Linc. I'll come right home," she told him before hanging up.

Brigid was a little surprised, because Linc was usually the calmest guy around and rarely got upset. How could this one couple get under his skin so much? Brigid decided it would probably be best if she stuck around the B & B this weekend to help keep Linc calm.

The couple would be leaving on Sunday, so all they had to do was stay out of it until then. Brigid mentally said a prayer for the couple's stay to go smoothly and that everyone would start getting along.

"I better get back, I guess there was some sort of situation at the B & B," Brigid said as she reached for her purse.

"What do you mean?" Fiona asked, concerned. "Was it that couple?"

"Yeah," Brigid said. "I guess the guy was being mean to his wife, and Linc is ready to do something drastic. I need to get back so I can calm him down." She stood and turned to her sister. "Your designs are amazing. You're amazing. You'll knock their socks off, just wait and see."

"Thanks," Fiona said as she gave her sister a hug. "I needed to hear you say that."

"Don't even mention it," Brigid said.

"If Linc needs help, let me know," Brandon said as he set Aiden down, who promptly took off for his room. "If this guy is bad enough to make Linc mad, I can only imagine what's going on."

"Thanks," Brigid said. "I hope the next couple of days go better.

Otherwise, I feel like I may have to have a talk with Sheriff Davis to see what my options are."

"Remember," Fiona said as she walked her sister to the door. "You don't want to get a reputation for being a busybody, but you also don't want to allow people to act like jerks under your roof. That's a pretty fine line you've got to walk."

"I know," Brigid sighed. "I just hope this blows over quickly."

She hurried out to her car and got in it, Jett by her side. She never thought this kind of thing would be a problem she'd have to face when they opened the B & B. But now the reality was setting in. Would she and Linc be able to handle this couple or would the couple do something to injure the B & B's reputation?

CHAPTER SIX

Ed Hawthorne finished washing his dishes and dried his hands. Once again it had been a long and quiet day. He spent most of his mornings down at the local cafe with the other older members of the community, drinking coffee and talking. Then he'd stop by the post office, check his mail, and head home to watch some TV until dinner, which usually consisted of one of those frozen, instant meals or something else that was quick and easy to prepare. After he did the dishes, he'd watch a little more TV or occasionally read a book.

Day in and day out, it was almost always the same. Every time he stood at the sink to clean up after himself, he could hear his wife's voice from beyond the grave. Maybe it was just wishful thinking, or perhaps her spirit really did look after him. Whatever it was, he welcomed it, but at the same time, it always reopened the wound of her loss all over again.

"I could never get you to wash a single dish and now look at you," he almost always heard her say in that chastising but playful way of hers. Barb's eyes would twinkle and sometimes she'd lightly slap him on the shoulder for good measure. It had become a game of him not helping her with the dishes after their many years together.

Now all he wished was that she was here and he could help her, see her smile, or touch her hair. But it was that mischievous twinkle in her eyes that he really missed. Just one more moment with her was all he wanted. One more moment to see her that way, so he could hold onto that image for the rest of his life.

But Ed was a realistic man. He knew that wasn't possible, but sometimes he felt his wife was near when he hugged his daughter, Amanda. It was as close as he could get to holding Barb again, at least in this lifetime. They'd struggled with infertility issues, and Amanda had been their only child.

After years of trying and failing to have a child, Amanda had come along and changed everything. She was the light of their life and the very thing that had pulled Barb out of her depression over not having children. If it hadn't been for Amanda, Ed wasn't sure what would have happened to his beautiful wife.

Returning to his favorite chair, he slowly lowered himself into it. The evening news came on and he let out a low grumble. Picking up the remote, he began to surf the channels to see what else was on. Ed didn't like watching the news anymore. All they seemed to show these days were stories of sadness. People being hurt, places being robbed, more proof that the world was going down the toilet.

He didn't need to turn on the TV for that. The only reason he turned it on in the first place was to escape, and the news was most certainly not an escape.

Ed looked at the photo on the wall above the television of Amanda and her husband Brett. They were a very attractive couple, and he admitted they'd probably give him adorable grandbabies, but he didn't like Brett. Barb had seen it first, before he'd even had an inkling that something could be wrong.

Thinking back, he was sure that most of it had been that he simply didn't want to see it. He didn't want to admit that his brilliant and fun-loving daughter could end up in a relationship like she had. But once he had a heart-to-heart talk with Amanda, he'd known. Brett was destroying his little girl.

The vibrant young lady he'd raised to speak her mind and be

proud of herself had changed dramatically. Quite simply, she'd become meek. She never did anything without checking with Brett first, and when he was around, sometimes that included speaking.

Ed had noticed a number of times when she seemed to look over at Brett to check and make sure it was all right for her to say something. That wasn't right, and Ed hated seeing her that way. When she was alone on her visits to his house she still would struggle, as if Brett had managed to find a way to make her fear him even when he wasn't around.

Ed had taken up where his wife had left off trying to convince their daughter she deserved more. He'd spoken with Barb about it in the hospital a day or so before she passed. Barb had been weak and had made him promise that he'd do whatever he could to not only convince Amanda of her worth, but also keep her safe. Ed had made her that promise while she was in what would end up being her death bed. He had no intention of going back on his word.

As he sat in his chair, thinking of his daughter, he realized he hadn't heard from her in a few days. He picked up the phone and dialed her number. He tried to speak with her at least once a week, just to make sure she was okay. After two rings, she answered.

"Hey, Dad," she said softly. "How are you?"

"I'm good, peanut. I just thought I'd call to see how things are going." That was his innocent way of admitting he was checking up on her. Not that she ever seemed to mind.

"Uh, things are good," Amanda said. "Brett and I are going to be staying at the New Dawn B & B in Cottonwood Springs this weekend."

"Really?" he said, slightly surprised. "Isn't Cottonwood Springs a small town? Why are you going there?" A surge of worry shot through him. Things between Brett and Amanda had started getting fairly rocky according to the last conversation he'd had with Amanda when she'd come to see him. What if things reached a boiling point while they were in Cottonwood Springs? It was several hours away, too far for him to easily help her.

"I wanted to get away from things for a while, so I saved some money for us to take a short weekend trip. The place is new, and I thought it might be good for us to go somewhere quieter," she admitted. "Maybe we can straighten things out a little."

"Is he going to do anything nice for you since you're paying for a weekend trip for two? Or could I even hope that he's being romantic to my little girl?" Ed asked.

He'd seen and heard about how Brett didn't show Amanda much affection. Usually he was too engrossed in what he was doing to even consider doing something to show his wife that he loved her. To Ed, it seemed like Brett wanted a maid more than a wife. Actually, a slave might be the more appropriate term.

"Not exactly," she said. "If anything, I think it's made things worse." She said the last part much quieter, almost as if she were whispering.

If she was admitting that things were bad, then they had to be. What she thought was okay was often the complete opposite to Ed. "What do you mean?" he asked.

"Can't really say," she said. "But you never know, things might turn around." Her voice turned cheerful at the end and the pure hope she had in it broke his heart. How could she still have faith in a man who had proven time and time again he wasn't worthy of it? Not for the first time, Ed wished his little girl would have found a good man and not the pathetic excuse for one she'd saddled herself with.

"I wasn't calling for anything special," he told her. "I just wanted to let you know I love you and that I'm here if you need anything. And I do mean anything." He'd had a conversation with her before about leaving Brett. She knew where he stood. He'd made his views on the man very well known to her.

"I know, Dad. I appreciate it. I'll call you when we get home from our trip, okay?" she said.

"Okay, honey. But I want to know what happened, you hear?" There was no way he'd let whatever happened get brushed under the rug. If she couldn't deny it was bad, then he needed to know.

"Sure thing! Love you," she said cheerfully before hanging up.

Ed looked at his phone before returning it to its base. Something wasn't right. He had half a mind to drive over to her house and find out exactly what had his daughter talking in code. Because if she couldn't talk to her father in front of Brett, then maybe something needed to be done.

There was no way he was going to allow any daughter of his to be treated that way. She should be able to feel secure enough that she could say anything she wanted. There was no reason for her to be fearful at all. Especially not of her husband. Ed may be old-fashioned, but he still believed that a husband should do all he could to make sure his wife felt loved and protected. Amanda should feel safe in Brett's company at all times, and if she didn't, maybe it was time for Ed to take steps to ensure she did.

"He better not have hurt her," he grumbled. "Because, so help me, if he's harmed one hair on her head, I will personally make him pay."

CHAPTER SEVEN

"We're having brioche French toast this morning," Brigid said as their guests sat down at the table. "I hope that's okay with all of you." She was in a great mood for that early in the morning and was hoping to have an even better day. The sun was shining, the birds were chirping, and they had guests in the B & B. Why wouldn't it be a great day?

"I haven't had French toast in forever," Amanda said wistfully as she settled into her seat.

"Then I hope you enjoy," Brigid said politely as she filled everyone's glasses with orange juice.

"Growing up, my favorite breakfast food was French toast," Eric, the other guest who was currently staying at the B & B, said.

"Mine too," Amanda said with a grin. "I'd make my mom cut it into triangles, and then I'd dip them in a bowl of syrup. I always became a sticky mess, which was probably why she didn't make it very often."

Everyone chuckled politely. Brigid silently hoped that whatever had been going on between Brett and Amanda had passed and now they could have a calm visit. Perhaps Linc interceding helped give Brett a little perspective on how he was acting, so he could correct his behavior.

That would actually be a very good thing she decided. What better advertisement than a couple falling in love all over again at your B & B? Every relationship had its ups and downs, and these two were no different. They could have been struggling and had hoped this weekend would put them back on track.

"I'll be right back," Brigid said as she headed back into the kitchen. Linc was standing at the stove, pulling the first few slices off the griddle. Brigid gave him a quick kiss on the cheek as she peeked over his shoulder. "How's it going?" she asked.

"About ready," he said with a nod and then paused. "How's it going out there?" He seemed apprehensive, almost as if he was nervous about going into the other room.

"Good, I think,' Brigid said happily. "Everything seems to be just fine. I'm hoping that Brett and Amanda just hit a rough patch in their marital relationship, but they're working to mend things. You know how that can go. They seem to be in good spirits this morning."

"I'm glad," Linc said, sounding relieved. "I didn't want this weekend to go terribly for anyone. I'd hate to have guests leave unhappy, even if one of them does seem determined to make everyone else that way."

"Me neither," Brigid agreed. "I think it will all work out. We just have to keep the right attitude." She began plating each person's meal as it came off the griddle.

Working together, Linc and Brigid finished preparing the plates. They added a few slices of French toast to each plate and sprinkled them with powdered sugar. The result was simple, but elegant looking. Soon they were bringing everyone's breakfast out to the table. Brigid had a smile on her face as she returned, hopeful for the morning.

But when she came back in the room, the energy had shifted. Eric and Amanda apparently had a friend in common and soon they were talking as if they were long lost friends themselves. Brett looked anything but happy with the turn of events. He was sitting back in his chair with his arms crossed, watching them talk. To Brigid, the conversation seemed harmless, but Brett's attitude wasn't.

"Here you go," Brigid said brightly as she tried to level out the conversation. When she placed Amanda's plate in front of her, she said, "I hope that it's as good as you remember your mom's." She touched Amanda's arm lightly and gave her a slight smile. The young woman looked up and returned it with one of her own.

"This smells amazing," Eric said as he placed his napkin in his lap. "I've missed home-cooked breakfasts." He looked excited to get his first taste.

"Would anyone like some coffee or anything else to go with your breakfast?" Linc asked politely. He looked around at each person and they all shook their heads. "Wonderful. Brigid and I will get our plates and join you in just a moment." Amanda and Eric nodded while Brett remained stoic and still as a statue. Linc headed back to the kitchen and Brigid followed.

"Did you notice Brett?" Brigid whispered as they stepped into the privacy of the kitchen and picked up their plates.

"The way he seemed ready to explode as his wife talked to Eric? Oh yeah, I noticed it all right," Linc said angrily. He took a deep breath, as if he were trying to calm himself down.

"I think I may have spoken too soon," Brigid sighed. All her hopes for a romantic weekend for the couple had just gone up in smoke. Maybe this was just one of those couples whose marriage couldn't be saved? Brigid usually tried to hold out hope for almost any situation, but she knew that sometimes things were too far gone to be turned around.

She began to wonder if there was anything she and Linc could do to help change that. Even if it was something as simple as making one day for them relaxing and enjoyable. At this point, she'd consider that a win.

"We should just act hospitable but stay out of it as much as possible," Linc said as much to himself as he did to Brigid. "Obviously, we try to keep the peace, but we should do our best to not get involved."

"Who are you telling? Me or yourself?" Brigid asked with a raised brow.

"I'll admit I'm saying it more for my benefit. There's something about the whole situation that's rubbed me wrong. I'm seeing my old coworker in it. But I also see Holly. I think about what I'd do if my daughter was being treated that way. I don't think I'd be able to hold my tongue." He looked down at the plate he was holding in his hand and frowned.

"But we have to," Brigid reminded him. "You're right, we need to keep the peace in our place of business, but at the end of the day, they are strangers, and we can't insinuate ourselves into their personal affairs. They aren't Holly. Holly has a good head on her shoulders and a great boyfriend."

"But it could be," Linc pointed out, slightly frustrated. "You know it as well as I do."

Brigid nodded. She knew he had a point, but she couldn't focus on that. If she did, she was fairly sure she wouldn't be able to keep her mouth shut. "I do. But I just keep telling myself that Amanda's not our responsibility."

"Are you trying to sleep with my wife?" Brett's raised voice cut through their conversation. Brigid and Linc looked at each other wide-eyed before grabbing their breakfast plates and hurrying back to the table.

"Hey, man," Eric said with his hands raised. "I'm not…"

"Don't give me that," Brett growled. "No man takes an interest in a woman like you're doing unless he's trying to get in her pants." Meanwhile, Amanda was red-faced and unsuccessfully trying to get Brett to calm down. Her hand was on his arm, but she might as well have not even been there for as much good as it was doing.

"How does everything taste?" Brigid asked loudly as she entered the room and sat down at the table. Brett fell silent but continued to stare menacingly at Eric while he ate. His eyes were filled with fury that he was barely able to contain. Brigid was thankful he had enough sense somehow to keep a lid on it.

"It's wonderful. Thank you so much," Amanda said sweetly. Her eyes darted around as she tried to decide how much Brigid and Linc had heard.

"It really is," Eric said, while keeping an eye on Brett. His gaze wasn't filled with as much anger as being watchful. There was no fear in his eyes either, which made Brigid nervous. If these two grown men decided to go at it, they could do some serious damage to each other. The last thing she wanted was to have to call Sheriff Davis on her guests.

Brigid began to make small talk with the guests as they ate and the tension in the room seemed to subside, but just slightly. She kept the conversation light and Linc sensed what she was doing. He joined in and soon Amanda and Eric also joined them in the conversation. Brett wasn't as amenable and answered questions with as short of an answer as he could. When Brett was finished eating, he seemed eager to leave the table.

"Would you like me to carry this to the kitchen?" Brett asked Brigid with a forced politeness as he held up his plate. Linc watched Brett, but didn't say a word.

"No, that's okay," Brigid said. "Just leave it there, and I'll get it in a little bit."

Brett gave a curt nod and turned to his wife. "I'm going for a drive. I'll be back soon," he said before placing a kiss on the top of her head, his eyes still on Eric. His gaze spoke volumes, and Brigid knew she was going to have to keep an eye on him or there would be trouble.

"Okay," Amanda said carefully.

"Are you looking for anything in particular in town?" Brigid asked. "Would you like me to give you some directions?"

"Not really," Brett said as he pushed in his chair. "I told Amanda I wanted to see what Cottonwood Springs had to offer. This seems like the perfect time. I think I need a little air."

"Enjoy," Brigid said as Brett strode toward the front door, his keys in his hands. Once he was in his SUV and pulling away, Amanda finally spoke.

"I'm so sorry he caused a scene," she said. "He just gets a little possessive sometimes. He doesn't mean anything by it."

Brigid and Linc exchanged glances. "You do realize that's not healthy in a relationship, don't you?" Brigid asked.

"I know," Amanda sighed. "But I'm not sure what to do about it." She bit her lip nervously as she kept her eyes cast down on the table.

"If I may butt in," Eric said from across the table. "I'm a veteran, and I've seen this behavior in some guys I knew from when I was in the military. It's not good, and it only ends up getting worse. It might be next month, next year, or five years from now, but those bad behaviors grow. People like that are a powder keg just looking for a spark to set them off.

"Don't be afraid to reach out for help. It's vital that you know where you can turn and what to do if you need some help." Eric was giving her such a tender look that it touched Brigid. She could tell this young man was speaking the truth and from his heart.

"It's not like he hits me or anything," Amanda said, still not looking up. "But he's gotten so controlling. I guess it kind of snuck up on me. And then at other times he'll be so nice to me. He'll say things like he can't live without me or that he can't function without me."

"That's still another form of control," Linc said, speaking up. "That's how they do it. They convince you that they'd hurt themselves or others if you leave. Tell me, what do you think he'd do if you left him?"

"Oh, I could never...," she began.

"Yes, you could," Brigid said softly. "You could leave."

Amanda's eyes widened. "No, I really don't think I could. He's said things. I don't want to repeat them, but I'll just say that I don't think it would be a good idea."

Brigid got the feeling they'd pushed as far as they should, so she bit back the response she wanted to give Amanda and instead took a drink of coffee. She had to maintain boundaries, even when everything within her was screaming otherwise, because what she really wanted to say was that if anyone made you feel like you were trapped, then no matter how nice they could be, you should run.

"If you'll excuse me," Amanda said. She stood up from the table and hurried to her room, quietly shutting the door.

CHAPTER EIGHT

Eric Newberry was sitting on the bed in his room at the B & B, still a little in shock over what had happened at breakfast. Not that he was afraid for himself. He admitted he found Amanda attractive and may have slightly been flirting with her, but not because he was trying to make a move on her. It was just the way he was.

Eric was a light-hearted, fun-loving guy who had a tendency to smile a little more or be a little more interested when the person speaking was a pretty lady. If that was a crime, he was happy to commit it. Besides, it seemed as though Amanda could use a little attention.

Eric had heard them through the walls. He wasn't at the B & B much, since he was here mainly to visit family, but he was around enough to have heard Brett speaking to his wife in a way she didn't need to be spoken to. That's all he had to know. He'd seen enough mistreatment of women while he was serving in the military in a combat zone to last him a lifetime.

Over there, men didn't care about women and their feelings, and as a man who had grown up with three sisters, that didn't sit well with him. It also made him prone to be more compassionate towards women and the struggles they faced on a daily basis. When he was younger, he hadn't been aware of some of the behaviors men used to control women, but once he'd had more life experience, he couldn't stop from seeing them. It was like a sickness that had been spreading in society.

Kicking back on the bed, Eric did his best to forget about breakfast. Anyway, he'd be driving over to his parent's house soon to meet up with them so they could all ride together to go see his grandmother. She was aging and had recently expressed an interest in having a family reunion. The whole family thought it would be nice to drive up to where she lived and surprise her, especially with Eric in town. She'd be excited to see her grandchildren together.

It was still a little before the time Eric had to leave, so he decided to step outside and get a little fresh air. He walked out of his room and heard Brett and Amanda speaking with raised voices across the hall. His heart hurt for the couple, realizing they were having a tough time.

Brett seemed like a jerk, but Eric didn't know what they'd been through together. He always did his best not to pass judgment when he didn't know the full story, although Brett was making it a little hard for him to do that. Brett's anger made the situation much more difficult.

He peeked around the corner and saw Linc and Brigid in the kitchen, cleaning up after breakfast. Linc was singing softly as he wiped the counters down and Brigid swept the floor. Their big black dog was laying on the floor just outside the kitchen. He lifted his head, mildly interested in Eric before putting it back down on his paws and closing his eyes.

Eric had never been around a dog quite that big before, but he had to admit in his short stay at the B & B he'd become a fan of the dog. If he ever settled down and had a house of his own, he could easily imagine having a big dog like that laying around.

When he stepped outside, he took a deep breath of fresh mountain air. Back in Florida, things just smelled differently than they did in Colorado. He never realized how much he missed the scent of the mountain air, but once he arrived back home, it had hit him like a ton of bricks.

He thought it was interesting he'd been around the world and still his very favorite place to be was right here in the mountains of Colorado. Funny how life works out that way. Just coming back here made him consider relocating. Maybe not back to his home town, but perhaps somewhere in the state.

Eric circled around the house, noticing the benches that had been scattered around for guests, so they could sit and relax. He sat down on one in the shade of the house and pulled out his phone. There was an e-book he'd started reading on the plane that had caught his attention, and he really wanted to finish it while he was here. When he got back home and was caught up in the swing of his normal life, he didn't know when he might have a chance to finish it.

He quickly got lost in his book and was startled when Amanda appeared around the corner of the house, breathless and looking emotional.

"Oh, I'm sorry," she said quickly. She turned to leave.

"No, wait," Eric said as he stood. "Please, don't leave."

She froze in mid-step, as if his words had forced her to go against her will.

"I don't want to cause any more trouble for you. I really am sorry about breakfast. He just gets a little...," she struggled to find the right word.

"Psycho?" Eric offered and she smiled.

"Not what I was going to say," she clarified.

"Maybe not," he said shrugging. "But I would. Please, come and sit. I'm just killing a little time until I have to leave."

"What are you here for?" she asked as she sat down on the bench.

Eric decided that maybe it was best if he remained standing.

"Family," he said simply. "And you?"

"Romantic getaway," she said rolling her eyes. "As you can obviously see, it's not going so hot."

"Apparently," Eric said. "I'm sorry if our conversation caused any trouble for you. I was just trying to be friendly."

"No, it's not your fault," Amanda said. "He's like that a lot anymore. It seems no matter what I do, it triggers some sort of argument these days. It wouldn't matter if it was you, someone else, or even no one, he would have found a reason to act that way. He always does."

"I'm sorry to hear that," Eric said sincerely. "I'm actually a counselor, so may I offer some advice?" Amanda nodded, so he continued. "Often there's some kind of an event that triggers this sort of behavior in couples. I'd be willing to bet you two have had some problems before now, but there was probably one event that seemed to really push things into a new dimension. If you figure out what that is, maybe it can help you narrow down what the root of the problem is."

Amanda smirked. "I know exactly what the problem is. I haven't been taking his attitude with a smile anymore. I've started fighting back."

"Are you sure that's safe?" Eric asked, concerned. "Not that I'm telling you to lie down and take it. But sometimes that's a little like teasing the tiger."

"Honestly, I don't know," Amanda admitted and then shook her head. "I probably shouldn't be talking to someone who's practically a stranger about this."

"Remember, I'm a counselor. I typically only work with people who have PTSD, but I can make an exception." Eric had a good sense of intuition when it came to knowing when someone needed to talk. If anyone needed to get things off their chest, it was Amanda. "I promise that whatever you tell me will be confidential."

She sighed. "I've talked to my dad about some of what's happened, but I really wish my mom was still alive. But then again, I probably wouldn't tell her either, because I know she'd worry. She'd push me to leave or something." She shook her head and looked at the ground.

Eric leaned against the house with his shoulder. "And why don't you if you think that's what you should do?"

"To be honest, I'm afraid," she said simply. "He's said things that made me feel unsafe."

"You should never stay where you don't feel safe," Eric instructed. "There's a reason you're having those feelings. Don't push them down and hide them. Uncover them and face them."

"Amanda," they heard Brett's voice nearby.

"I better go. I don't want anything else to happen. If he sees us talking…," she said quickly as she stood up. "Thank you."

Eric nodded as she hurried in the direction of her husband's voice. The fearful look in her eyes as she retreated caused something deep within Eric to rise up. Suddenly he saw her as more than just a pretty woman.

She was someone's daughter, maybe even a sister or niece. How would he feel knowing a woman in his family was in this situation? Knowing that she felt trapped and couldn't do anything. He'd want someone to help her, if he couldn't.

"I thought I'd find you around here," Brett's low voice snarled as he came around the building. "Are you still sniffing around my wife? I thought I made it clear you should stay away from her."

"Nothing's going on. Just polite conversation," Eric said as he held his hands up. He certainly wasn't afraid of Brett, but he didn't feel the need to start trouble either. Eric had already experienced enough physical conflict in his life. He didn't want any more.

"I think you're trying to move in on her," Brett said as he drew closer. "Are you trying to get my wife in bed?" He was far too close to Eric now, and Eric's years of training wanted to kick in and subdue this man. He deliberately took a slow and steady breath to calm his nerves.

"Why are you so overbearing about Amanda? Don't you see that you're crushing the life out of her with the weight of your demands?" Eric asked as he squared his shoulders. Some bullies just needed someone to hold a mirror up to their actions.

"I demand that she act like a wife," Brett growled. "And I think you should watch yourself."

"Is that a threat?" Eric said with a smile. "Because I have to tell you, I'm not someone who takes kindly to threats." He knew he shouldn't talk like this, but Brett definitely needed to be put in his place. Maybe he always used intimidation to get his way, but that wouldn't work with Eric. He'd stared death in the face before, and this man wasn't even close to being as frightening as that.

"You can think of it however you want to," Brett said with a cocky lift to his chin. "But let me tell you this, if I catch you sniffing around my wife again, you'll pay for it."

"Looking forward to it," Eric said, his anger getting the best of him.

Brett took a step back and then made a slicing motion across his throat as an unspoken message to Eric who simply smiled in response. He must have really gotten under the man's skin for him to be threatening him like that. Good. That means at least for now that the focus was off of Amanda.

Eric knew there was nothing he could do when they left, but while they were at the B & B and in his sight, he was going to do whatever he could to try to help Amanda. He'd keep an eye on Brett and intervene if needed and in whatever way he saw fit.

Brett was a train wreck waiting to happen, that was for sure, and if he was going to hurt anyone, Eric was going to make sure it wasn't Amanda, even if he had to take matters into his own hands to stop it. It's what he'd want someone to do if it were one of his sisters. So for now, he was going to look out for her as if she were his own family, which meant that Brett better watch his step. One wrong move and Eric would have no trouble dealing with the brute in whatever way was necessary.

CHAPTER NINE

"Then I told Levi that if anyone is going to get perks from Fiona landing this clothing line deal, it's going to be me," Holly said with a laugh as she and Brigid sat on the swing between their house and the B & B.

It had turned out to be a nice afternoon and they were taking advantage of it by sitting outside while the dogs played and ran around. Lucky had started a game where he would run under Jett and pester him just enough to cause Jett to want to chase him. Then, when he realized the little dog was too quick, he'd stand in one place, which caused Lucky to start the game all over again.

"I'm just glad to hear you and Levi are still talking to one another," Brigid said with a smile. "After that whole ordeal that you two went through with the Oracle, I wasn't too sure the two of you would remain friends."

"I wasn't either," Holly admitted. "But it didn't take long for him to come to his senses. Especially once the sheriff returned his money and told his parents what had been going on. They hadn't realized just how out of place he'd been feeling. But I think things are going to change now." Holly watched the dogs running around with a satisfied look on her face.

"I hope so," Brigid said happily. "He's too good of a kid to go down the wrong road. Like I said, I was really worried that your friendship might have taken a hit. You two went through a lot together dealing with that Oracle character. I'm happy it turned out all right in the end."

"I'm just glad Linc didn't keep me grounded for the rest of the summer like he said he would. Then I could have had problems fixing things up with Levi. Kind of hard to repair a friendship when you're practically under house arrest." Holly chuckled as she watched Jett flop over on his back to fend off Lucky's onslaught.

"I wasn't sure how long he was going to keep you on lockdown, either. I think it may have helped when Fiona pointed out that I've done the same sort of thing."

Brigid had done her best to help plead Holly's case, but Linc had been determined to stick to his guns, and she wasn't going to be the one to step on his toes. But Brigid knew that what Holly had done was something she would have done herself if she'd been in the same situation. It was hard to be mad at someone when they're following your lead.

"I get it," Holly nodded. "It was a bit reckless, but it all worked out, so I don't see any point in getting too upset now. I certainly learned a lesson, though. It's not like I'm going to repeat that mistake."

"Good," Brigid said, satisfied. "That's what counts. I don't want to have to go through anything like that again. You scared some years off of me when I got the call that you were in trouble."

"If things had gone right, you wouldn't have. But I guess that's the way it goes sometimes." Holly turned toward the B & B. "Looks like we've got company."

Brigid turned to see Amanda and Brett heading their way. She hated the fact that when she saw Brett, she got a knot in her stomach. In her book, the man was trouble. Simple as that.

"Good evening," Brigid said as she greeted them. "Can I help you with something?"

Brett approached them first with Amanda a respectful two steps behind him. "Actually, we were curious about the woods back there," he said as he pointed to the nearby treeline. "I enjoy walking around in the trees, so we were wondering if it would be okay if we went back there. I don't plan on causing any trouble. It just looks like a nice area to relax in."

"Oh," Brigid said as she turned around and looked at the treeline. "I know that a lot of it is our property, but there's no fence or anything to separate it from our neighbors' property. Linc could tell you for sure where it ends. He has some way that he uses to determine where ours ends, but I can't remember what it is for the life of me. Do you Holly?" she asked as she turned towards her.

"I don't, sorry," Holly admitted. "I just know that it's not terribly far in."

"Linc's somewhere around here if you want to ask him. Actually, I think he's out in front." Brigid was a little leery of sending the man in search of her husband, but she didn't have much choice.

"Okay, thanks. We won't make a mess or anything. You won't be able to tell we were even out there. I just like to be surrounded by trees. It's soothing to my nerves," he said simply. "Thank you." He turned and began walking towards the treeline as his wife hurried to follow him. She gave Brigid and Holly a slight smile as she scurried after him.

"Well, that was a little odd," Holly said after they were far enough away.

"Everything about that couple is odd," Brigid sighed. "That man got into it with Linc during breakfast and then with our other guest. He's got a temper on him, that's for sure."

"Really," Holly said. "What's his deal?"

"I'm not sure," Brigid answered. "He seems very controlling over his wife and a bit edgy. He accused our other guest of trying to sleep with her. He took off this morning and left her behind. He said he just wanted to drive around. He ended up coming back later like he hadn't even caused any trouble at breakfast."

"I'm just trying to wrap my head around someone getting into it with Linc. He's like, the most civil and level-headed guy I've ever known. My mind is just blown away." Holly turned and looked at the couple again. "Must be trouble in paradise, because it looks like he's really not happy with her for some reason."

Brigid turned and saw that they were almost to the trees and Brett had turned to face Amanda. It looked as though she might be crying, and Brett was waving his hands around. They were far enough away that Brigid and Holly couldn't hear what was being said, but their body language spoke volumes.

"Come on, let's go inside," Brigid said as she stood. "I don't like feeling as if I'm watching someone deal with their dirty laundry."

Holly nodded and stood up, following Brigid towards the B & B.

Brigid wasn't sure what to do with the couple. Part of her felt that she should reach out to her friend, Sheriff Davis, but she also felt a certain reluctance to get law enforcement involved. She didn't know Amanda's situation or what their home life was like. What if Brigid called the sheriff and then it turned out to be nothing?

They might post angry reviews of their stay at the B & B and that wouldn't help their fledgling business. She decided the best thing she could do would be to keep it to herself, but also watch out for Amanda. If she saw or heard anything that truly sounded as if Amanda was in trouble, Brigid would be there for her. Right now, all she could do was have the woman's back while she was a guest at the B & B. At least then Brigid would feel she'd done all she could.

When she entered the B & B, she began to do what she considered "closing down" for the evening. It was a process of making sure everything was picked up in the kitchen and put away. Then she topped off the water pitcher in the fridge, in case the guests were thirsty at night. Holly went along behind her, helping where she could, both of them working in silence.

"Do you think that woman is going to be okay?" Holly finally asked in a quiet voice.

"I don't really know," Brigid admitted. "She seems like someone who could use a friend."

"Yeah, she sure looks that way," Holly said, nodding in agreement.

"This is probably one of the hardest things about dealing with the public," Brigid said with a deep sigh. "You get to see glimpses into people's lives, and sometimes it might be at a time that's difficult for them. But all we can do is try to help them while they're here with us and wish them well when they leave. With any luck, maybe they'll come back to visit, so we can see what happened."

"Yeah, I guess," Holly said, sounding distracted.

"I'm going to head back home, you coming?" Brigid asked.

"Not yet. I need to check on the dog food situation over here. I'm going to the store tomorrow, and I think we need to get some." Holly hitched her thumb over her shoulder towards the back porch where they kept the dog food for the B & B.

"Okay. I'm going to take a shower and get in bed. See you in the morning." Brigid wrapped her arms around Holly and pulled her in for a hug.

"Goodnight," Holly said as she squeezed her back.

Brigid turned and left Holly at the B & B while she headed back to the house. She was more than ready to call it a day. Rather than going straight to the house, she remembered she'd left her glass of tea out by the swing, so she decided to grab it on the way home.

She paused while she was at the swing, wondering if Brett and Amanda were still arguing. She looked over to where she'd last seen them, but they weren't there. She prayed silently for the couple to find peace in whatever way that was right for their situation. She didn't exactly want Amanda to stay with Brett, but she also didn't like to judge people when she'd only met them a couple of times.

As she headed for the back door of the house, she crossed her fingers that tomorrow would go smoother than this morning. The sounds of the summer evening soothed her nerves a little as she crossed the yard.

Maybe tomorrow I'll be able to start that book I've been meaning to get to, she thought. *I've only had it sitting on my nightstand for a week and I really want to read it.*

Between reading for her job as an editor and helping Linc run the B & B, it had been quite a while since she'd had time to sit down to read anything for pleasure. But she'd picked up an interesting looking book the last time she'd been to Fiona's, and she'd been itching to get to it. Perhaps tomorrow would be slow enough she could do just that.

CHAPTER TEN

The next morning found Brigid at the B & B with Linc and Jett, starting breakfast. Jett was pacing back and forth at the back door, whining. This was somewhat strange behavior for him as most mornings he was already on his first nap of the day by this time.

"What's wrong, Jett?" Linc asked as he stepped around the counter to get a good look at him. "You already went to the bathroom. Do you need to go again?" He joined the big dog at the door and opened it for him. Rather than dash out, though, Jett looked up at Linc and whined again.

"What's his problem this morning?" Brigid asked from where she was standing at the counter. She'd just taken some streusel coffee cake muffins she'd made out of the oven, and she couldn't stop what she was doing to see for herself.

"I'm not sure," Linc said as he looked down at the big dog. "I think he's trying to tell us something."

"Come help me with the plates, then," Brigid told Linc. "As long as he's not planning on having an accident in the house, it can wait. It's almost time to serve breakfast to our guests. We can figure out what he's trying to tell us after we get this out of the way."

Linc nodded, joined her at the counter, and started plating the breakfast meal. Brigid preferred that he did it, because he put so much care and artistry into it. He'd even started buying greens and other garnishes to decorate the plates. "Hopefully today will be a calm day. I did so much yard work yesterday, I'd like to kick back and do a little reading."

Brigid gave him a pointed look. "You, sit down and read? I'll believe it when I see it." She chuckled as she turned the burners off and Linc gave her a mock offended look.

"I read, I'll have you know," he said indignantly. "I read threads on the internet…" he gave her one of his grins that always made her stomach do a little flipflop.

"You're something else, Linc Olsen," she said with a chuckle. And of course, that was why she loved him. He was strong and reliable, but also playful and funny. It seemed like he was always up to something.

"That I am," he said proudly as he began to pick up the plates. "Come on, Jett," he said happily, "Maybe I'll share some of my bacon with you," but the dog didn't move. Instead, he stayed where he was, staring out the window in the door.

"Jett, want to watch us eat breakfast?" Brigid called, hoping to pry the dog away from the window. Instead, he continued making an anxious pacing movement as he stared outside.

"Huh," she said. "He's really acting strange." As they started walking out of the kitchen she said, "Speaking of strange, did you hear that sound last night? Sounded like a gunshot or something."

Linc shook his head. "I didn't hear anything. When did you hear it?"

"I'm not really sure. I think you were in the shower," she said. "I meant to say something about it to you, but I was too sleepy to remember when you finally came to bed."

"Who knows. Probably just someone scaring off a wild animal," he said. They stepped into the dining room and saw Amanda and Eric, but there was no sign of Brett.

"Where's Brett?" Brigid asked, feeling hopeful that he'd decided to sleep in. "Isn't he joining us for breakfast?" She began placing the plates in front of their guests.

"I-I'm not sure," Amanda said as she fidgeted with her napkin. "He never came in last night."

Brigid paused before she sat down. "What do you mean?"

"We had a heated discussion yesterday evening, and I left him alone out by the trees. Since he didn't come in last night, I think maybe I made him mad enough he went somewhere else." She cast her eyes downward toward her plate.

"I can make a few calls around to see if he's checked in somewhere else," Brigid said, trying to reassure Amanda. "I'm sure we'll figure out where he went."

She tried her best to make it sound like it was no big deal, but she was worried. What could he be doing? Where could he have gone? It was hard to say since she didn't know what Amanda had said to him, but Brigid hoped he'd just gone somewhere to blow off steam. She couldn't remember if she'd seen their SUV parked outside this morning.

"Sometimes we men just need some space," Linc said with a kind smile. He and Brigid exchanged a look that said they were both concerned.

Amanda nodded. "Yeah, maybe that's it." She continued to fidget and took a few small bites of her breakfast. She pushed her eggs around as she took small nibbles of the bacon and muffin. "This - coffee cake muffin is really delicious. I wish I could do it justice."

Eric and Linc began talking and Brigid allowed herself to get lost in her thoughts. She wasn't exactly disappointed that Brett wasn't at the breakfast table. He was so domineering towards Amanda that it was awkward to be around them. Hopefully, he'd decided to part ways with his wife and went to stay somewhere else. If they couldn't get along, it was probably for the best.

He could have spent the night at the B & B run by their friend, Rich, or at a motel in town. She hoped wherever Brett was, he stayed there. Although Brigid had had her fill of him, something about the situation didn't seem right. However, for now, she was more than willing to just roll with it.

Brigid watched Amanda as she pretended to eat. Her eyes were red-rimmed with dark circles beneath them, as if she hadn't slept a wink. Her heart ached for the woman, and she silently sent up another prayer to whoever was listening that the woman could get free of her abusive husband.

Whether Amanda wanted to admit or not, that's what he was. Even if he'd never laid a hand on her, the result was almost the same. Amanda was afraid of her husband and what he might do next. No matter what spin you tried to put on it, it was traumatic to Amanda, and no one deserved to be treated like that.

As everyone finished up their breakfast, Brigid turned to Amanda and asked, "Where was the last place you saw Brett?" Both Linc and Eric turned to hear her answer.

"By the treeline out in back," Amanda said nervously. "We were just inside the trees. Not too far."

Brigid nodded. "I'll go see if I can find any trace of him out there and which way he may have gone, before I make a few calls. That way I'll have an idea where to look first." Eric excused himself and left the room. Linc began carrying dishes to the kitchen.

"Look," Brigid said softly to Amanda when they were alone, "I want you to know you're safe here. Is there anything I should know about what happened between you two last night?"

Amanda shook her head. "I don't think so. I kind of stood up to him, and he didn't take it well." She looked as though she wanted to say more, but refrained.

Brigid nodded. That was enough for the time being. "Go see if you can get some rest, and I'll let you know what I find out, okay?"

Amanda nodded and headed to her room. Her shoulders were hunched over, and Brigid was almost certain she heard her sniffle as she walked away. Brigid collected the last of the dishes and joined Linc in the kitchen.

"I don't know if you should go looking for him by yourself," Linc said. "Maybe I should go."

Brigid shook her head as she set down the plates. "No, if he's in one of his ugly moods, I don't want you to get into it with him. So far, I'm the only one he hasn't been angry with. The last thing we need is to have him accusing you of trying to sleep with his wife. That really wouldn't look good if he were to leave a review."

"What's going on?" Holly asked as she stepped into the kitchen, Lucky hot on her heels. "Why is Jett standing at the back door like that?" They all turned to see that Jett hadn't moved from his post at the door.

"I don't know," Brigid said. "And one of our guests never came in last night. I'm going to go look for him."

Holly nodded. "I'll help Linc while you go do that," she offered.

Brigid nodded. "Okay, I'm going to walk back in the woods and see if I can find out anything. I'll take Jett with me and try to figure out what's going on with him. Maybe he lost a toy out there or something. When I get back, I'll call around and see if Brett's checked in somewhere else."

She left Linc and Holly to clean up the breakfast dishes and joined Jett at the door. "Do you have something you want to show me?"

she asked the well-trained dog as she twisted the door handle and pushed the door open.

Jett took off through the door, jogging ahead a few yards before turning around and waiting for Brigid to catch up. He did it several times. Going just far enough and then turning around to wait for her to join him.

"You crazy dog," she said shaking her head. As she walked, she wondered what really happened last night between Amanda and Brett. If he didn't come back last night, well... that just didn't seem to fit his personality. Since he seemed to be so worried about her staying under his thumb, why would he just take off and leave her alone?

Sure, he'd taken off yesterday morning after breakfast, but that was only for an hour or so, not all night. Something wasn't right, but Brigid tried to convince herself that it was probably because she didn't really know the couple. Maybe he wasn't as controlling as he'd seemed. She knew first impressions could be deceptive. Most likely, he'd wanted some rest and no more arguing.

Finally, she came to the edge of the trees. Jett had waited for her, but now he nudged her hand, as if to get her attention.

"Yes, yes," she said looked down at him. "I'm listening. What is it?"

Jett turned and began to sniff as if he was searching for something. He seemed to have gotten some scent, because he lifted his nose from the ground and began walking. It wasn't his usual slow, lumbering gait, but was instead far more purposeful, almost driven.

That was what caught Brigid's attention the most. Jett was usually slow, calm, and relaxed. Something was definitely up. There was a reason he was acting this way and it was up to Brigid to determine what it was.

"What is it, Jett?" she asked in a voice almost too quiet to be heard. A surge of fear shot through her. Why was she so uncomfortable? It was only Jett and her out here. She looked down at the ground, and it was clear that someone had passed this way. There were freshly broken branches and small rocks had come loose from someone walking across them. She followed Jett farther into the woods, towards a little dip in elevation. That's when Jett came to a stop.

Brigid hurried forward, wondering what it was that could have made Jett so insistent that she had to come all the way out here. She rounded a downed tree and saw someone's feet stretched out on the ground. Unable to help herself, she took a few more steps and saw the rest of the body, Brett's body. She gasped. It definitely was Brett, and he had a bullet wound in the side of his head.

She turned away quickly, her hand over her mouth. Forcing herself to take slow breaths, she took a few steps backwards and stood, trying to steady herself. Jett bumped up against her reassuringly. "We have to go tell Linc and call Sheriff Davis," she said to him. "Come on." She began walking as fast as she could back to the B & B. "Of all the times not to have my phone with me," she said to herself in exasperation.

CHAPTER ELEVEN

Brigid rushed back to the house, Jett trotting beside her, thinking about Brett. The unmistakable stillness of his body on the ground had shocked her. Why, she wasn't sure. It wasn't the first dead body she'd seen. But her hands were trembling as she reached for the door to the B & B and twisted the door knob. She let Jett precede her through the door before entering and shutting the door softly behind her.

"So?" Linc said as she came into view. He and Holly were washing dishes together, and he didn't look up from the sink. "See anything?"

"Yeah, we have a problem," she said softly.

"Oh?" Linc said as he looked up. Seeing her expression, he dried his hands. "What's wrong?"

Brigid crossed the short distance to stand as close to him as possible. "Brett's dead."

"Are you serious?" Linc asked as Brigid turned toward the kitchen island and reached for her phone.

"Unfortunately, I am," she muttered as she picked up her cell phone and searched for Sheriff Davis' number. Linc and Holly stared at each other, dumbfounded. They couldn't believe what she'd just said.

"What can I do fer ya', Brigid?" Sheriff Davis asked as he answered her call.

"I have a situation over here at the B & B," she said quickly. "One of our guests has been shot. He's out back in the woods. He's dead." She was doing her best to take calm, even breaths. Otherwise, she was afraid she'd start hyperventilating.

"Self-inflicted gunshot or otherwise?" he asked, getting straight to the point.

"I'm not really sure," she admitted. "I didn't stay there and look that long."

"On my way now. Don't tell anyone besides Linc if ya' can help it. Let's keep this under wraps fer now," he said. "Don't want anyone gettin' worked up if it was done by their own hand."

"Will do," Brigid said as she hung up.

"Are you sure it's him?" Holly asked with a horrified look on her face. She'd been waiting for Brigid to get off the phone so she could ask.

"Pretty sure," Brigid nodded. "I admit I didn't exactly stand there and analyze his features. But I would say with a fair amount of confidence that it's him." She closed her eyes to take a deep breath and saw a flash of the scene in her mind. Quickly, she jerked her eyes back open to keep from seeing anymore. "I wonder how Amanda is going to take this."

"Well if he's as bad a person as you said he was, maybe she won't be so upset," Holly shrugged. Brigid and Linc looked at her in surprise. "What?" she asked as she looked at them. "You can't tell me you weren't thinking about it. If he really was as domineering and abusive as you say..." She let her sentence trail off.

Linc leaned closer and whispered, "What if she did it?" His eyes darted from Brigid's to Holly's and back again.

Brigid's mind was racing, trying to process these new developments. What did this mean for their B & B? Would people think it was unsafe to stay with them because one of their guests had been murdered? And what if he hadn't been murdered? What if Brett had taken his own life?

It wasn't out of the realm of possibility. Maybe his own guilt over how he'd been acting had been too much for him. From the little Brigid knew, he seemed unstable. Perhaps that's what Amanda had meant when she said she couldn't leave him? There may have been a time when he'd told her he'd take his own life if she left him?

"We'll just wait until the sheriff gets here," Brigid said finally. Her mind kept going back to last night when she'd heard the gunshot. If she would have known...

"Didn't you say you heard a gunshot last night?" Linc asked almost as if he were reading her mind.

"Yeah, I think it was around the time you were in the shower," she said distractedly.

"Are you sure?" Holly asked. "I thought I heard something last night too."

"I don't really know," Brigid admitted. "I was reading, but I was really tired, so I could be wrong. Maybe someone else heard something to help us narrow down the time. But let's not get ahead of ourselves. Maybe Brett took his own life? I hate to say it, but at this point, that's the best we can hope for."

"Why's that?" Linc asked.

"Because if he didn't, then that means we had a murderer in our backyard last night," Brigid said ominously. "Come on, we better go keep an eye out for the sheriff. It shouldn't take him long to get here."

The three of them headed out front, the dogs following close behind. As soon as they shut the door behind them, the sheriff's truck rounded the corner and came into view. An ambulance without its lights on wasn't far behind, followed by another sheriff's department vehicle.

Brigid approached the sheriff's truck as Sheriff Davis stepped out and walked around it to where Brigid was standing.

"I'd say good mornin'," he began, "But don't think it's gonna' be so good today."

"No, it's not looking like it," Brigid admitted. She remembered hoping it would be a peaceful morning after all the drama the Stephensons had created around the B & B. Apparently, it wasn't over.

"I called backup and told 'em to be as quiet and discreet as possible," Sheriff Davis said. "Ya' don't need any more attention brought to this than need be." He adjusted the gun on his belt as he spoke.

"I appreciate it," Brigid said. Deputy Keegan exited the other sheriff's vehicle and came over to where they were standing.

"Where's the body?" she asked. That was one of the things Brigid liked about her. She didn't mince words and was really good about getting directly to the point.

"If you go straight back from the house, there's a little hill just inside the woods," Brigid said as she pointed towards the forest. "He's just past it. The yard should be dry enough you guys can just drive right on back to it. It's a long way to be walking back and forth for anything you may need."

"Thank you," Deputy Keegan said with a nod. Her blonde hair was damp and pulled back into a French braid. From the way she looked, Brigid assumed she'd just gotten to the station when Brigid had called.

"Do you know who the guy is that you found out in the woods?" Sheriff Davis asked as they began to walk towards the B & B.

"Brett Stephenson. He and his wife are staying with us. They've been having a, uh, tense weekend," she said as she struggled to find the right words. Deputy Keegan stopped at the ambulance and spoke with them before she headed to her own car.

"Tense how?" he asked. They joined Linc and Holly on the front porch. Sheriff Davis nodded to them in acknowledgment as he tapped his brown sheriff's hat. The other vehicles slowly drove past the B & B through the yard.

"He seemed to be a bit overbearing," Brigid said. "I hate to make assumptions, but I thought she was afraid of him."

"I see," he said with a nod. "I wanna' take a quick look at what ya' found before I do anythin' else. Mind if I drive back there and have a quick peek?"

"Do what you need to," Linc said matter of factly. "I'm not going to worry about the lawn in a situation like this."

Sheriff Davis turned and headed back to his truck as they sat down on the porch. Linc and Brigid took a seat on the swing, reaching for each other's hand while Holly quietly sat in one of the other chairs. Lucky jumped up in her lap as she looked down at the ground. Brigid felt her heart ache at the distracted look on her face. If only Holly had been at work, she could have been spared this. Holly was a strong girl, but even the strongest person is shaken when someone loses their life.

They sat silently, waiting for the sheriff to return. Meanwhile, Brigid's investigative mind was beginning to kick in. She needed to make sense of what had happened and the only way she knew to do that was to uncover clues. Like how convenient it was that Brett's wife was the last one to see him alive as far as she could tell?

And it wasn't as if they seemed to have a good relationship. Had Amanda finally had enough and put an end to her overbearing husband? Or was it like they'd imagined earlier? Maybe Brett had threatened to hurt himself if his wife wanted to leave. When she'd given him an ultimatum and walked away, perhaps he'd decided things were over between them. Anything was possible, and Brigid hated not knowing.

The sheriff's truck soon reappeared and he drove back onto the street. When he joined them, Sheriff Davis looked grim.

"You were right. Found some ID on the body and his name is Brett Stephenson. So he was stayin' here with his wife?" he asked.

"Yes," Brigid said. "She's inside."

"Have ya' spoken to her 'bout this?" Sheriff Davis asked as he pushed his hat back and scratched his head.

"No, I haven't," Brigid admitted.

"I'll save ya' the trouble. Jes' show me where she is," he said simply. "Anyway, officially it's my duty."

Brigid nodded and led him into the B & B. The sheriff followed her down the hall to where she stopped in front of a door. She paused, realizing that the sheriff was about to change Amanda's day completely. Actually, her life. Right now, she was probably in there resting and imagining that her husband was somewhere else and would be back soon. In a moment, she'd know and everything would change.

"His wife is Amanda Stephenson. This is their room. I sent her to rest while I was looking for him, because she looked as though she hadn't slept a wink last night. She told me he hadn't come back to the room, and she'd been worried," she said in a voice just above a whisper.

Sheriff Davis nodded and knocked lightly on the door. After a moment, Amanda slowly opened the door. Her eyes seemed redder than they had been before and widened when they saw the sheriff.

"Amanda, this is Sheriff Davis. He has news about your husband." Those were the only words Brigid could think of to say. There was no way to prepare the woman for what she was about to hear.

"Oh, okay," she said as she opened the door farther.

"I'll be out front," Brigid told Sheriff Davis, and he nodded before she walked away. She didn't want to be there for the conversation that was coming if she could help it. There was no way she wanted to tell Amanda her husband was dead. But what if she already knew? What if she's the one who did it?

That was one thought she couldn't stop herself from thinking. After all, why not go to a completely different town to do it? A place where no one knows their history. If she could make it look like a random crime, maybe Amanda thought she could get away with it.

And as much as Brigid hated to admit it, she felt sorry for Amanda. What if she thought killing her husband was her only way out? Every day you read about women who felt trapped by an abusive partner.

She breathed deeply as she stepped back out into the warm sun and looked at her family. Hopefully, this wouldn't end up negatively affecting them. All she could ask for was that Sheriff Davis could find out who had done this and get it wrapped up quickly.

CHAPTER TWELVE

"Can I speak with ya' two privately?" Sheriff Davis asked as he returned to the porch. Linc and Brigid looked at him and then at Holly.

"I'll take the dogs back to the house. They could probably use a treat," Holly said as she stood up and led them away. Sheriff Davis waited to speak until she was out of sight.

"Here's the deal," Sheriff Davis said as he took the seat that Holly had vacated. "Brett Stephenson didn't take his own life. Almost certain we're lookin' at a murder."

"Are you serious?" Brigid gasped. She'd been telling herself that it was a suicide, and to hear the sheriff say otherwise was a blow. It also caused her to think once more about Amanda. Could the woman have it in her to take the life of her husband? And if it wasn't her, then who had done it? And the Stephensons weren't even from Cottonwood Springs.

"Ain't no gun back there, makin' it impossible for him to have done it to himself. I asked his wife if there was anyone who had somethin' against him or that he'd argued with recently," the sheriff said as he looked directly at Linc. "She tol' me you and the other guest here both exchanged words with him. She insisted she didn't believe either of ya' did it, but she wanted to be honest and answer the question."

Brigid gasped and looked at Linc before turning back to the sheriff. "Surely you don't think Linc did this?"

Sheriff Davis hung his head. "Look, ya' know I gotta' cover all the bases and play by the rules. Deputy Keegan said they're thinkin' the time of death was somewhere around the 9:00 p.m. mark. What were ya' doin' 'bout that time last night, Linc?"

Brigid turned towards Linc. Her heart was beating a million miles an hour. Wasn't that when he was in the shower? Or was it before? She couldn't be sure and suddenly she was very worried about her husband.

She remembered him saying something about going to double check that he'd put away the leaf blower, but she couldn't remember when that was. Could Linc have had enough of the man and not told her? Could he actually be capable of killing another human being?

"I remember it was around 8:30 when I took a shower," Linc recalled. "Right after that I told Brigid I had to go make sure I'd put all my yard equipment away. I'd done both yards and couldn't remember if I'd put everything away. That was probably around 8:45. It couldn't have taken very long because I didn't see anything out on the porch where I'd set it all, so I turned around and came back inside. I grabbed a glass of ice water and stood in the kitchen drinking it."

"That's right," Brigid gasped. Now she remembered how it all happened. "I heard what I thought was a gunshot, but didn't think too much of it. The house is fairly well-insulated, so sometimes things sound different. I just shrugged it off as a car backfiring or something and not even a minute later Linc was walking into the bedroom."

"I personally didn't hear anything, but I wasn't paying any attention. Besides, I was opening cabinets, cracking ice, things like that. Come to think of it, I ended up getting a snack for Jett and me,"

Linc said.

Brigid turned and looked at him in shock. "What?" he asked innocently. "It was a peanut butter cookie, no big deal." He turned back to the sheriff. "After that, I went to our bedroom and Brigid was dozing off. I gave her a kiss and went to bed."

"I'd assume it'd take a man your age longer to run back up to the house than that. Plus, you woulda' at least been breathing heavy," the sheriff pointed out.

"My age?" Linc said with mock surprise. "Why, I'm no older than thirty-five," he teased.

"I highly doubt anyone could run that fast," Brigid said as she shook her head. "Sorry, Linc makes jokes when he's worried."

"That's okay," Sheriff Davis chuckled. "I've gotten used to it by now. I didn't really consider ya' a suspect, Linc, but I had to get yer' whereabouts anyway. Ya' know how it is, jes' standard operatin' procedure. I don't wanna' skip any steps and get accused of favoritism. Elections are comin' up soon, ya' know."

"I do," Brigid nodded. "Which is why I don't think you should dismiss the possibility that Amanda may have done it." She lowered her voice, not wanting Amanda to hear her.

"Oh? Why do ya' say that?" Sheriff Davis asked. "Already considered the possibility, but I'd like to hear what ya' have to say about it. Especially since you've been around 'em the past few days."

"Their relationship seemed strained," she began. "Right from the moment they showed up things seemed off between them. He seemed extremely overbearing. We dismissed it simply because we didn't know these people or their situation."

"Understandable," Sheriff Davis nodded. "People argue, that ain't a crime."

"No, it's not," Brigid agreed. "But we began to notice that things weren't normal between the couple, like him yelling at her and making a scene."

"Are you referrin' to when the victim had a disagreement with Linc and the other guest?" he asked.

"Yes," Brigid nodded. "Linc, tell him what happened."

Linc began to tell the story about being out in the shed and hearing Amanda crying and stepping out to intervene. "He seemed to be looming over her, like he was using his height and position to make her feel smaller."

"So ya' think he was tryin' to intimidate her?" the sheriff asked.

"Exactly," Linc nodded.

"I'll have to speak with yer' other guest to find out where he was and what's occurred between them," Sheriff Davis said.

"I'm fairly sure he's left by now," Brigid said. "He has family living here in Cottonwood Springs, and he goes to see them every day. But we were both witnesses to what happened between Brett and Eric. That's the guest's name."

Brigid went on to recall the morning when Brett accused Eric and Amanda of flirting when all they'd been doing was having a friendly conversation. "It was as if Amanda felt the need to pacify him at all times and make excuses for him," she said.

Brigid continued, "It was like he was a ticking time bomb she had to tiptoe around so he didn't explode. The fact that she and the victim went walking in the woods a few hours before he was murdered doesn't look so great for her either."

"I'm wonderin' if perhaps somethin' was going on between yer' two guests, Eric and Amanda. Maybe Eric wanted Brett outta' the way?" Sheriff Davis said.

"I guess it's possible. They do seem to have hit it off, but I never really noticed anything that seemed romantic in nature," she mused.

"I don't know," Linc said softly. "I think I may have seen something in his eyes. It could have been nothing, or it could have been the beginning of something." He shrugged. "Hard to say."

"Do you have any contact information for Eric?" Sheriff Davis asked. "I'd like to speak to him as soon as possible."

"Sure," Brigid said. "I can log into the system and pull that right up." Brigid stood up and the sheriff followed. Her heart had slowed marginally, knowing that Linc was cleared of suspicion, but she was still worried. Somewhere in their tiny town was a killer, and they'd committed their heinous crime in her backyard. There was no way Brigid was going to sit back and let someone get away with that.

CHAPTER THIRTEEN

"Here you go," Brigid said as she handed the slip of paper with Eric Newberry's phone number on it to the sheriff. Sheriff Davis pulled out his phone and began dialing the number.

"Mr. Newberry?" he asked. "This is Sheriff Davis with the Cottonwood Springs Sheriff's Department. I got a matter I need to discuss with ya' in person. Is it possible for us to meet somewhere?" He paused, listening to Eric on the other end. "If that ain't a problem, I'd be happy to. Okay, then. I'll see ya' in jes' a bit." He hung up his phone and turned to Brigid. "Ya' wanna' ride with me? See if anythin' seems off with him?"

"Sure, not a problem," Brigid said with a quick nod.

"Let me send a message to Deputy Keegan so she knows what's goin' on," he said as he began to text on his phone. "The coroner can take the body, but I want her to stay here and keep an eye on the wife. Jes' in case."

Brigid nodded. "That's probably smart, at least until we have more details."

They both headed back out onto the porch where Linc was waiting for them.

"We're going to go see what Eric was doing last night," Brigid told him as he stood up when they approached.

"Okay, I'll stay here and hold down the fort. I doubt he did it, but I understand you've got to check every possibility." Linc looked toward the door to the B & B with apprehension.

"That's right," Sheriff Davis nodded. "But don't worry. Deputy Keegan will sit with ya' once she's done with the crime scene area. Do me a favor and make sure Amanda don't leave. Not only jes' in case she's our suspect, but because she really shouldn't be unsupervised for a while."

"Sounds good," Linc said. "Hurry back." Brigid gave Linc a quick kiss before she and the sheriff walked out to his truck.

"If I didn't know ya' better, I'd swear ya' were a magnet fer trouble," Sheriff Davis teased.

"I don't think I'd disagree with you," she smirked, "So I guess I might as well embrace it."

They climbed into his truck as Brigid wondered at the turn of events that had just taken place. She didn't want to think Eric had anything to do with Brett's murder, but she was smart enough to know that people weren't always what they seemed. Beyond their cordial conversations at breakfast, she hadn't really had much of a chance to find out much about him, since he was always gone.

Didn't he mention something about having been in the military? That almost implied that he may have taken a life before. Had he felt that he needed to again? It may not have been for himself. Maybe he and Amanda really had acted on some sort of chemistry between them, and he wanted to free her from her husband's grasp. Brigid was fairly sure she'd seen some true crime stories on TV that ended that way, so it was a plausible motive if all that was true.

"What's yer' feelin' 'bout all this?" the sheriff asked as they drove through town.

"Honestly, I don't know. Nothing seems to make sense. The obvious choice would be that Amanda did it, but I certainly have no evidence," she admitted.

"Why do ya' think she did it?" he asked. "Got anythin' specific?"

Brigid thought about it for a moment before shaking her head. "I don't know. Just a hunch, I guess. Maybe it was because she seemed so scared of him. I agree with the line of thinking that someone did this to protect her, so I'm not entirely sure she did it. And yet, at the same time, it's logical.

"She doesn't seem to reach out for help, so I have no idea who else it could be. Granted, we're all strangers, but she struck me as someone trying to keep her husband's acts a secret, and at the same time, trying to keep his anger from affecting others. Besides, they live a few hours away. If someone was going to kill Brett because of the way he treats her, why wait until they came here? Why not do it back home?"

"All valid points," Sheriff Davis said. "But sometimes things like this jes' ain't logical. Murder is often somethin' done in the heat of the moment. I'm leanin' towards her as our suspect. She's the most logical one, and she's the only person here locally that he was tied to. Unless there was somethin' to Brett's accusations."

"What do you mean?" Brigid asked.

"When Amanda spoke about this other guest, Eric, she seemed different. I'm willin' to bet somethin' happened there," he said, his eyes still on the road.

"Really?" Brigid asked. "I haven't seen them talk except at breakfast."

"Don't mean it ain't happened," he said cryptically. Brigid fell silent, wondering if he was right. Had something gone on between Eric and Amanda that she hadn't noticed? Could the answer to what occurred in their backyard be right under her nose? She hoped not.

Eric seemed like a good guy. He was polite and friendly as well as loving towards his family. Brigid crossed her fingers he wouldn't be the one who had pulled the trigger.

A short time later, she and Sheriff Davis were standing on the porch of a nicely kept home on the fringe of town. The house was an older, small farmhouse. The porch was covered in the green fake grass that Brigid hated and had never understood why people bothered to spend money on it. A pair of rocking chairs sat lazily in the sun.

Sheriff Davis raised his hand to knock on the screen door, but paused when the interior door opened. Eric Newberry appeared in the doorway. "Please, come in," he said politely.

They stepped inside, and the living room was just as clean as the outside of the home. A worn couch was covered in plastic and an older woman sat in a nearby chair, knitting.

"Who is it?" a woman's voice called out from the kitchen.

"Don't worry, Mom. It's for me," Eric answered.

"I'm Sheriff Davis," the sheriff said as he extended his hand. Ya' already know Brigid. What ya' may not know is that she works with me on occasion."

"No, I didn't know that," Eric said, surprised. "Good for you, Mrs. Olsen."

"Please, call me Brigid," she said.

"Sit down," Eric said, gesturing to the couch. He pulled up another chair as the older woman continued to knit. "How can I help you? Has something happened?"

"First thing I gotta' do is ask ya' where ya' were around 9:00 last night," the sheriff said, cutting straight to the point.

"Nine?" Eric asked. When the sheriff nodded, he began to think, then he turned to the kitchen, "Mom, do you remember what time I left here last night?"

A woman with light brown hair stepped out of the kitchen and paused. She seemed surprised to see a uniformed officer sitting on the couch. "Um, I think almost 11:00. Why? Are you in trouble, Eric?"

"We're just coverin' all the bases, ma'am," the sheriff clarified. "So you can vouch that he was here that late? Anyone else here?"

His mother put her hand on her ample hip. "Well, my sister was here and so was one of the neighbors. We're having a family reunion later today, so we've been busy. Actually, there were a number of people here." The older woman continued knitting and ignored them.

"What's happened?" Eric asked, looking at Brigid.

"Brett Stephenson was found murdered in the woods behind the B & B this morning," Brigid said. "We're attempting to piece together everyone's whereabouts that he's been in contact with."

"Amanda's husband? The jerk?" he said, sounding surprised.

"Is that the woman you told me about?" his mother asked.

He looked at her and nodded. "Mom, it smells like something's burning."

"Oh, darn," she said as she hurriedly went back into the kitchen.

"Did she do it?" he asked quietly.

"Who?" Brigid asked.

"Amanda," Eric said softly. "Did she kill him?"

"We don't know yet," the sheriff said interjecting. "Ya' know somethin'?"

Eric looked conflicted. "Well, maybe. I know I have to tell you, since it's a murder investigation, but I swore I wouldn't speak about it."

"We won't tell anyone else," Brigid said. "But we need to know everything."

"I spoke to her the night before last. It was late at night, and I'd just come in. She was sitting on the front porch of the B & B. I ended up talking to her for a while. She'd been crying, and I couldn't leave her out there alone. I was raised better than that." Eric shook his head and looked at the floor.

"She told me how she was afraid of her husband and how he'd told her once that if she ever tried to leave, he'd kill her. She was terrified of him, but she was determined to give him an ultimatum this weekend while they were away. She wanted him to straighten up and treat her right, or she was gone. But then, something happened."

"What?" Brigid asked.

Eric paused. "She kissed me. I didn't pull away either. We were talking and I was trying to help her out, giving her advice. I told her she was too beautiful to be afraid for her life. That she deserved to be put on a pedestal and treated like a queen. That's when she leaned over and kissed me. I probably should have pulled away, but I couldn't."

"What happened then?" Sheriff Davis asked.

"She apologized and ran in the house. The next morning, she acted as though none of it had happened," he shrugged.

"So she was planning on leaving him," Brigid mused aloud.

"That's what she said," Eric shrugged. "I don't know how it went or if she managed to get the courage to tell him."

"Thank ya'," Sheriff Davis said. "If I got any more questions, I'll let ya' know. If ya' think of anything else, gimme' a call. Here's my card with my contact info on it." The sheriff stood up and Brigid followed him.

"Will do," Eric said as he followed them to the door. "I hope you catch whoever did it, even though it seems they did her a favor."

"Sure seems that way, don't it?" Sheriff Davis said as he stepped outside. Brigid stepped out beside him as Eric shut the door behind them. They walked back to the truck, and when they were inside, the sheriff continued. "So she put a move on Eric and then suddenly her husband ends up murdered?"

"Yeah," Brigid said as she buckled her seatbelt. "I was having the same thought. Seems pretty suspicious."

"That it does," he said as they pulled away. "But I still think it's too simple. Too neat. Granted, she may not have thought it completely through, but it don't feel right. Why now?"

"Exactly. Doing it here makes her look like the murderer. There has to be something we don't know about. Maybe once we get back to the B & B, there will be another clue or something to help clear it all up," Brigid suggested.

"Perhaps," Sheriff Davis said. "Or perhaps she jes' didn't think it through at all."

"I guess that's always an option," Brigid admitted. "I just don't like it."

"Ain't never a good thing when someone dies. Sometimes the crimes hit a little too close to home and it's easier to see where the lines blur. But the fact of the matter still remains that there is a line. We gotta' do what's right if someone crosses that line," he said. "Even if we don't like doin' it."

CHAPTER FOURTEEN

The Sheriff and Brigid climbed out of his truck after they pulled up in front of the B & B. The coroner's van was gone and Deputy Keegan was sitting on the porch with Linc. Even from a distance, Brigid could tell Linc was worried. His usually square shoulders were slumped, and he was looking down at his feet as he and the deputy talked. Jett and Lucky were with them, Jett laying on the porch, and Lucky sitting beside Linc.

"Did ya' find anythin' else?" Sheriff Davis asked Deputy Keegan. Brigid silently hoped they'd found an amazing piece of evidence that would lead them right to the killer. Granted, she knew that was wishful thinking considering the state that Linc was in, and her heart broke for him. This couldn't be easy on him.

It wasn't that long ago that they'd been dealing with someone messing with the website for the B & B right before the grand opening. That had been stressful enough, but this? This was something else altogether.

"I did," she nodded. "I found a bullet casing and what looked like footprints. I took pictures and sent them off to Williams so he can do a little research on them. At least this way, he might be able to find out what the murder weapon was. He said he'd get back to me as soon as he could.

"I found one good solid print that I've put plaster in to see if we can get any details from it. I'll need to check on it in a few minutes. I'm hoping with what we learn from those two items we can begin to build a profile of our killer."

"Good work," Sheriff Davis said. "So far it looks as though the other guest is cleared. Seems he and the victim's wife may have had a moment the other night. Don't think he did it, but it puts a new perspective on the victim and his wife's relationship."

"Really?" Linc asked as he looked to Brigid. "That's interesting. I never would have guessed that."

Brigid nodded. "He told us himself. I'm willing to bet they spoke more than either of them let on, although that's certainly not a crime. How's Amanda doing?" Brigid asked.

"She's sleeping right now," Deputy Keegan said. "I just went to check on her and she was out like a light on your couch. I think she was trying to wait for you, but sleep got the best of her."

Brigid nodded. "I'm sure she needs all the rest she can get. She's such a sweet woman I hate to think she could be a killer."

"Don't know enough to decide yet," Sheriff Davis reminded her. "She may not be."

"I told Holly she could go ahead and head over to work," Linc said. "I didn't see any point in her sticking around here today. At least this way, she has a distraction."

Brigid nodded. "I think that was probably for the best. She'd just worry if she was here, and she'd want to get involved."

"That's what I thought," Linc agreed.

"Well, think I'm gonna' go take a good look at the crime scene. See if maybe I can make somethin' of it myself. Deputy, ya' care to join me?" Sheriff Davis asked.

Brigid smiled as the two of them began to walk around the house and head towards the scene of the crime. She knew they were still seeing each other in secret and taking things slow. She was just glad the sheriff had someone in his life. He'd been alone for so long and now he had someone he could talk to and who would understand the pressures and demands of his job.

"I'm worried what this might do to the B & B," Linc said after a moment. "We've been doing really well, but if word gets out our guest was murdered…"

"Don't worry, we'll figure this out," Brigid assured him. "Whoever did this had to have left clues. You heard Deputy Keegan. She found a bullet casing and footprints. That means they may have left more clues. We can't give up yet. Things happen. As long as we find out who did this and they're dealt with, our business should be fine."

"Am I a bad person for not feeling sorry for the guy?" Linc asked. "I mean, you saw how he was. I wish I had some pity for him, but I don't."

"I understand," Brigid said, nodding. "He wasn't exactly a kind and gentle soul, was he?"

"No," Linc said as he shook his head. "That Brett was not. I guess he probably wasn't that way all the time, though. I'm sure he had some redeeming qualities that we didn't get a chance to see. Now I guess we never will." They both fell silent, lost in their own thoughts.

Brigid sat down next to Linc and interlaced her fingers with his. She sensed the tension rolling off of him in waves, and she wished she could do something to make it go away. The only thing she could think of to help, though, was to find the killer. And right now, that wasn't something she could do.

They heard movement coming from inside the B & B and Brigid turned towards it. "I think Amanda may be up. I'm going to go see if she's willing to talk. Maybe I can find out something she didn't tell the sheriff."

Linc nodded. "Good luck, I hope you're right. We need some help to make sense of what happened. I'll be right here."

Brigid went inside with Jett following, moving quietly in case she'd been mistaken about Amanda waking up. If the woman was still asleep, she didn't want to disturb her. As far as Brigid was concerned, even if they did have their suspicions about her, Amanda was still innocent until proven guilty.

However, that didn't mean Brigid wouldn't keep a sharp eye on her until they knew more about what had happened. When she looked towards the couch, she saw Amanda sitting up and simply staring off into space. Either she was still waking up or she was in a daze over the day's events.

"How are you?" Brigid asked as she slowly approached Amanda. Jett followed closely. She watched Amanda as her eyes blinked slowly, and she seemed to come back to herself.

"Okay, I think," she said. "I feel a bit more like myself now that I've gotten a little sleep, but I still can't believe it." A single tear rolled down her cheek. "We had our problems, obviously, but still..." It wasn't necessary for her to finish her sentence. Brigid understood what she was trying to say.

She crossed the room and sat down on the couch beside Amanda with Jett following her. At first he stayed beside Brigid, but his eyes never left Amanda. Slowly, he started inching closer to her. He sniffed her knee cautiously, and she reached out to touch him.

"He's really a huge dog, isn't he?" she said absently as she petted him. Jett seemed to be a welcome distraction for her, so Brigid allowed him to do what seemed to be instinctual to him.

"That he is," Brigid said softly. "He's a gentle giant, and he has a heart of gold." She paused, knowing what she wanted to say, but trying to find the right words. "Amanda, would you like to talk? I know I'm practically a stranger, but I don't have to be.

"I promise I've got a good shoulder to cry on. This is a time when you need a friend, and since you're not at home, I'm willing to be here for you, whatever you need."

Brigid was having a hard time seeing Amanda as a suspect considering everything the woman had been through and the behaviors that Brigid had seen. But on the other hand, how many women eventually snapped from cruel behavior? Physical abuse may leave physical scars, but emotional abuse left scars no one could see. Sometimes those were the most painful, because not everyone even believed they were real.

"I think I may be done crying," Amanda said softly. "Earlier, a lot of that was shock and sleep deprivation. I don't do well when I don't get enough sleep. Brett always said as emotional as I could get, I wouldn't make a very good mother."

"I don't think that makes you bad mother material. I think it just makes you human," Brigid pointed out. "There's plenty of people out there who struggle with being moody when they don't get enough sleep. That's just how some of us are made," she said reassuringly.

She couldn't believe anyone would ever tell someone they supposedly loved that they'd make a terrible mother. What kind of monster said something like that? They lapsed into silence as Amanda continued to stroke Jett's soft, black fur.

"Is he really... dead?" Amanda finally asked. "Like, for sure?"

Brigid nodded. "I found him myself. Well, with a little help from Jett here." She looked down at her dog fondly. He'd helped her more than she'd ever expected when she got him. Her heart swelled with pride to have him as a member of her family, knowing she could always count on him.

Amanda looked down at the big black dog who had rested his head on her leg as she absently petted him. She didn't lift her eyes from him as she began to talk. "Brett wasn't always like that. When we first met, he was a gentleman."

"What changed?" Brigid prompted. She wasn't sure where this was going, but she'd let Amanda say whatever she needed to say. Brigid knew that sometimes people just needed to get things off their chest.

"I'm not sure," Amanda said. "I've asked myself that very question so many times, but I've never found the answer. Sometimes I convince myself it's my fault." It looked as though she was talking to Jett rather than to Brigid, because of the way she was petting Jett and staring into his eyes. But that didn't bother Brigid in the slightest. She knew sometimes it was easier to talk to an animal than a human. They always seemed to be better listeners.

"Why would it be your fault?" Brigid asked.

"He never liked it when I talked to men," Amanda began. "I had a part-time job at a flea market, because it was all I could get at the time we met. Times were tough, and I had to move back in with my parents after college. To make a long story short, I had to quit work because he was jealous of the men who would come in and talk to me."

"You're a pretty woman, and that comes with the territory," Brigid said. "He should have known that would happen."

Amanda continued talking. "I started taking care of everything around the house, because I was living with him and I wanted to be useful. I didn't like sitting around doing absolutely nothing. But it was like he expected that from then on. When I started slacking off, he was sure I was having an affair.

"I couldn't even take my phone into the bathroom with me without accusations flying. I wouldn't go anywhere. I had no friends and no money, except what he gave me, and he still accused me of cheating."

"That wasn't your fault," Brigid told her. "It was his insecurities and his issues. His problems had nothing to do with you. You can't live your life trying to make others happy. That's not how things work."

"That's what my mom said," Amanda whispered as she finally looked up. "She'd started telling me that she thought he was no good, but then she got sick. Once she was gone, it seems like I spiraled down into a deep dark hole. I didn't care about anything after that."

Brigid's heart ached for this woman, but once again she wondered if it wasn't possible that she may have murdered her husband. Brigid knew it was never right to murder another person, but in this case, she could see where a jury might find it almost understandable.

Listening to Amanda, what she was describing was her whole world systematically being taken over by Brett. He'd made her feel so bad about herself that her self-esteem had been shattered. Had she broken so completely that she only saw one way out, and that way out was by murdering him? Brigid wasn't sure, but for Amanda's sake, she hoped she hadn't.

CHAPTER FIFTEEN

The front door opened and Sheriff Davis stepped inside. "Oh, good," he said when he saw Amanda. "Didn't wanna' have to wake ya'. Need to speak with ya' a little more."

Amanda turned toward the sheriff. "Oh? About what?"

Sheriff Davis took his hat off and sat down in a nearby chair. "Ya' seemed to have forgotten to mention that ya' and Eric Newberry had a moment the other night."

"Oh," she said, looking down at her fingers. "I didn't think that was important."

"Everythin's important," he said. "Need to know as much as possible in order to find yer' husband's killer. Even the slightest detail could make a huge difference in findin' out who did this. I want to know everythin' that happened. Did ya' kiss Eric Newberry the other night?"

"Yes, it's true. I kissed him the other night. I don't know what came over me. I was sitting there one moment just talking to him and then the next, my lips were on his." Her cheeks flushed pink as she looked away, embarrassed. "I didn't want to say anything because I was ashamed. I'm a married woman, after all. I shouldn't have behaved that way."

"We're not here to judge you, Amanda. We just want to find your husband's killer," Brigid reminded her. If Brigid was being honest, she couldn't blame Amanda. She'd noticed how kind Eric had been to her at the breakfast table yesterday morning. From the way she described how Brett had treated her, Brigid couldn't blame her for reaching out to Eric. He was a handsome young man who had shown her kindness, something that had been lacking in her life.

"I know I told you he argued with Brett, but I don't think he did it," she said softly. "Eric seems too even-tempered to do something like that. I'm sorry if it seems like I wasn't telling you everything. That's not the case. I really have no clue who could have done this, so I'm a little taken aback and in shock."

Brigid watched Amanda and was surprised by the lack of tears. Sure, she cried earlier, but she admitted that it was due more to a lack of sleep than actual sadness. Perhaps she wasn't as upset over her husband's death as Brigid originally thought. But at the same time, it could be that Amanda was still in shock. Or maybe Brigid had totally misread everything and Amanda wasn't crying because she didn't feel any remorse.

"We got a few leads, so don't ya' worry about that," Sheriff Davis said. "Now I need to ask ya' what ya' were doin' around 9:00 last night."

"Me?" Amanda asked, her eyes going wide. "You think I did this?"

"Ain't sayin' that," the sheriff said carefully. "I'm jes' tryin' to do my job. Ya' admit yer' relationship wasn't ideal and that ya' kissed another man the night before. Wouldn't be doin' my job correctly if I didn't look into all the possible angles here. I'm asking everyone involved the exact same question."

Amanda considered what he'd said and nodded. "After I left Brett at the treeline, I came back to the B & B. I walked around to the front of the B & B and was going to sit on the front porch again, like I had the night before. I'd told my husband that he needed to start treating me with respect or I was going to leave him. He laughed at me and told me he'd treat me with respect when I earned it. To be honest, I was sitting out there waiting for Eric to come home."

Her face flushed again. "But as I was sitting there, hoping that Eric might come along, Brigid's daughter, Holly, came out. It was fairly quiet, and she must have figured out I was upset, so she came over to talk to me."

The sheriff turned to Brigid. "Can ya' call Holly and see if she's able to gimme' a statement?"

Brigid nodded. "I'll go call her right now." She went outside where Linc was still sitting and pulled out her phone as the sheriff continued to speak with Amanda.

"What's going on?" Linc asked as he watched her.

"I have to call Holly to see if she can speak with the sheriff. Apparently, she and Amanda were talking last night right here around the time of the murder." Brigid pulled up Holly's number and pushed the green button.

"Hey, how are things?" Holly asked as she answered. "Everything get cleared up yet?"

"Amanda says you were talking with her on the porch last night," Brigid said, cutting to the chase.

"Yeah, I was. Why?" Holly asked.

"The sheriff wants to clear her as a suspect. Is anyone there at the bookstore so you can leave real quick to give him a statement here? If not, I'm sure he can come to you. But I thought if you could leave, it would make things easier on him" Brigid asked.

"Sure, Levi's here. Just give me a few, and I'll head that way," she said before hanging up.

"If she didn't do it, who did?" Linc asked as she slipped her phone back into her pocket.

"I don't know," Brigid admitted. "Hopefully the shell casing and footprint will give us a direction to go in. Can you think of anyone else who may have been around here? Perhaps they had a visitor or something? Did someone come to see them while I was gone or anything that you know of?"

"No, nothing," Linc said shaking his head. "I wish there had been, but I don't recall anyone else. If they had visitors, they were good at hiding."

Brigid nodded. "You're right. I didn't think they did, either. After all, they are a couple of hours away from their home, and neither one of them mentioned knowing anyone here locally." Brigid paused. "But Brett did leave the other morning. Maybe he upset someone while he was gone. That's the only possibility I can come up with."

Linc shrugged. "I have no clue. We could ask around, but we also don't know where he went when he was gone. Cottonwood Springs isn't huge, but there are still a lot of places he could have gone."

Sheriff Davis came out of the B & B and joined Linc and Brigid. "Long as Holly's story matches Amanda's, don't think she'll be stayin' on the suspect list. Everythin' she's sayin' seems to fit in with the timeline we're buildin'."

"So now what do we do?" Brigid asked.

"I'm gonna' help Deputy Keegan at the station with our evidence once I talk to Holly. Keep an eye on Amanda, if you would. Maybe get her talkin,' see if she remembers anyone who mighta' had somethin' against her husband. There may be a link we're just missin.' Some small, subtle thing that we're overlookin' now, but somethin' that can crack this case wide open. Ya' know how these things go. Ain't always obvious where the next step lies."

"You're right," Brigid said, nodding. They heard Holly's car approaching. "When you leave, I'll talk to Amanda some more. Maybe some seemingly small thing will come up and help us out. Besides, that shell casing and the footprint might bring you the last piece you need to point you towards the killer."

"Let's hope so," the sheriff said as Holly climbed out of her car. They turned to watch the young girl walk towards them. "Like to think this would be an open and shut case, but it's startin' to not look that way."

"You wanted to see me, Sheriff?" Holly asked.

"Holly, Amanda Stephenson says she was sittin' on this porch last night when ya' came out from the B & B and noticed her. She said ya' came over and spoke to her for a l'il while. Is that right?"

Holly nodded. "That's right. We were sitting right there just talking about life, love, things like that. I told her she didn't need to put up with her husband's crap, and that he was just trying to control her. I told her I'd be praying for her to find someone who would treat her right and also praying that she could find the strength to leave him.

"She said she'd told her husband that he needed to start treating her right, kind of giving him an ultimatum. I told her if he didn't, not to be afraid to kick him to the curb. That's when we heard that strange sound."

"What sound?" Sheriff Davis asked, his brow furrowed under the bill of his wide brimmed hat.

"It was distant, like a pop or something. Not super loud, but it still echoed. Like it was close, but not so close that I could tell what it was. Of course, out here sounds tend to echo, so they seem like they're louder. I wasn't really sure which way it was coming from.

"Amanda heard it too and said that it was probably a car backfiring or something." Holly shrugged. "We just sort of dismissed it when we didn't hear anything else, you know?"

"You probably heard the shot," he said with a nod. "If she was with you and you both heard it, then she can't be the killer," Sheriff Davis said. "Thanks, Holly. Sorry I had ya' leave work fer this. I jes' wanted to keep an eye on her until ya' said somethin' otherwise."

"Not a problem," she said with a shrug. "I know I didn't really meet the guy, but I'm not sorry she's free of him. He really twisted her thoughts around. You might want to suggest she get some sort of therapy or something. Her self-esteem is pretty bad, like she might need a professional."

"Thanks, I'll see what we can do. Yer' free to go," he said before turning towards Linc and Brigid. "Think I'll head out too, see what I can find down at the station." Sheriff Davis waved to Linc and Brigid as he walked Holly to her car. Brigid hoped he was right. With a little patience and attention to detail, she was crossing her fingers they'd find out who did this.

"This is just blowing my mind," Brigid said as she sat with her husband. "How could someone here in Cottonwood Springs have something against a man who doesn't live here? How could he get so angry at someone that quickly that they'd be willing to murder him?"

"I'm not sure," Linc admitted. "But I gotta' tell you the guy was about as pleasant as a splinter. You never know what he may have said or done to somebody. And who knows? Maybe we're looking at this all wrong? Maybe it wasn't someone with a personal vendetta against him."

"Are you saying someone just happened to randomly choose Brett of all people to murder? And in our backyard?" Brigid asked incredulously. "Linc, that seems like a bit of a stretch."

"I hope not, but nothing is making any sense at this point. Come on, let's head inside. We'll tell Amanda she can stay here for a little while on us. She doesn't need to have anything else to worry about at the moment," Linc said as he slipped his hand in Brigid's. They interlaced their fingers and he pulled her to her feet.

"That's a great idea," Brigid said. "I know she said her mother is deceased, but maybe she has some family that can come help her. She needs a support system right now. Besides, I can't imagine her driving home alone. It seems like too much for one person to bear."

Brigid sighed. "I wish I could give her some hope that we'll find who did this to Brett. They may have had a rocky relationship, but that doesn't mean it's not traumatizing to her. She just had her whole world tossed on its head."

"You're right. So for now, we'll reach out and try to be her support system. Come on, let's go see what she needs," he said as he and Brigid stepped inside the B & B.

CHAPTER SIXTEEN

When Brigid and Linc went inside the B & B, they were surprised to see Amanda standing up, pacing around the living room, her cell phone to her ear. She was holding her hand over her eyes.

"I know, Dad," she said. "I think I'm still in shock. It's all just so overwhelming, but the people here are super nice." She paused, and then said, "Honest, you don't have to worry about me. I'm okay at the moment."

Brigid turned to Linc and smiled. She was glad Amanda had reached out to someone and was telling them the news. It was a good sign that she was able to deal with it. "Where's Jett?" Brigid whispered to him.

Linc pointed over to the corner where Jett was napping and Brigid nodded. With all the commotion, she hadn't even thought to keep an eye on him. She was grateful he was such a calm and slightly lazy dog, otherwise she probably would have lost him a dozen times by now.

"Okay, if you're sure. Bye," Amanda said into the phone and then sighed. "That was my dad," she said as she turned to them.

"Is he going to come and help you?" Brigid asked. She was hopeful Amanda's father would be able to help her sort everything out as well as help her with the next chapter in her life.

"Yes," Amanda sighed. "I think I'm going to need him. Now that Brett's gone, I'm on my own again." Her chin began to tremble and she put her hand over her face. "I'm sorry."

"Go," Linc said as he nudged Brigid forward. "I'll find something else to do for now."

Brigid nodded and Linc slipped back out the front door. Brigid crossed the distance between Amanda and her and opened her arms. The woman didn't even hesitate as she stepped forward, a tear slipping down her cheek. Brigid pulled her into a hug that caused a flood of tears to start.

"I feel so bad," she cried. "But mostly, I feel bad because I'm more relieved than sad. Does that make me a terrible person?"

Brigid guided her back onto the couch. "I don't know what your marriage was like," she said carefully, "so I can't presume to tell you what you should be feeling. I think if that's what's in your heart, then it's valid."

Amanda nodded. "I mean, I guess I'm a little sad. I think I'm more upset over the idea of all of the possibilities that are gone now. I wanted to have children and do the whole white picket fence thing. Now it feels like it all went up in a puff of smoke."

"Who says you can't still do it? I know it's too soon now, but you can always meet someone else," Brigid pointed out. "Your life didn't end just because Brett's did."

If anything, now you can try again, Brigid thought. *Find a man who will treat you right, instead of like a piece of his property.*

Amanda seemed to think about what Brigid had said as she continued to cry. They weren't huge tears followed by sobs, but rather the kind that slid down still cheeks from eyes filled with pain. Jett lifted his head, almost as if he sensed the woman needed reassurance and trotted over to her. This time, he pushed up on the couch between Brigid and Amanda, where he knew he wasn't supposed to be.

"Jett!" Brigid cried out as his large rump pushed her back. "What on earth are you doing?"

Amanda couldn't stop herself from laughing as he climbed up, licking her tears. "Oh, he's not bothering me one bit," she said through her tears.

"He knows he's not allowed on this couch," Brigid grumbled slightly, "But I can make an exception just this once." She knew he didn't normally behave this way, so it had to be his reaction to Amanda's grief. She couldn't really punish him for being empathetic.

Jett laid his head and paws on Amanda's lap and seemed to give Brigid a look that said "Sorry."

"He just knows I need some support right now," Amanda said to him in a voice normally used when people talked to babies.

Brigid scooted over as he found a comfortable place and laid down again. She shook her head at the spectacle he was making, but she had to admit she was proud of him. How many people could say they had a dog that always seemed to know what was needed, even when he was sleeping? The way he'd woken up and come to Amanda's aid was touching. He was certainly a special dog, but then she'd known that for a long time.

"I came in to tell you that you can stay here for another few days completely free of charge," Brigid said once Amanda was comfortable after Jett's invasion on the couch. "And when your dad gets here, we can put him up in one of the other rooms. Our next guests aren't coming for a bit, so it's no trouble."

"Thank you so much," Amanda said. "I'm sure he'll be exhausted by the time he gets here. It's roughly a three-hour drive, so he'll probably be ready to stretch out and relax. He's not a fan of long car trips. Actually, I was surprised when he said he'd be heading my way. I was just calling him to tell him what happened. I didn't really expect him to drive all this way on his own."

"Well, he probably wants to take care of his little girl. You've been through a lot already, and it's not over yet. I'm sure he's concerned about who did this to his son-in-law and wants to be here for moral support for you. I can't say that I blame him. Just be glad you have such a great dad who'd hop in his car and drive this far at the drop of a hat."

Brigid knew if Holly called and said something like this had happened to her, Brigid would be walking out the door as soon as she'd hung up. There wouldn't be anything in the world that could stop her from being by Holly's side, and more than likely, Linc would feel exactly the same.

They both loved Holly so much, and she wasn't even biologically theirs. But love didn't care about genetics and family was made up of more than just people you were biologically related to.

"I'll be happy to see him," Amanda admitted. "You and your husband are so kind, but it will be nice to have a familiar face around. I don't really want to go anywhere until I hear more from the sheriff. Do you think he'll figure out who did this?"

Brigid looked into Amanda's large, hopeful eyes and couldn't bear to give her anything but hope. "Sheriff Davis is amazing at his job. I've helped him with cases like this, and we've yet to come across a case that we couldn't solve. I don't see how this one would be any different. It may take some time, but neither one of us will rest until we find out who did this and make sure they're behind bars."

Amanda nodded. "I don't understand why someone would do this."

"Don't worry, I'm sure you'll find out in time," Brigid said as she patted her hand. "It may not be today or tomorrow, but usually when we find who did it, we also find out why they did it."

Both women looked up when they heard Linc's voice say, "Hi,

may I help you?"

Brigid hoped it wasn't someone who wanted to book a room without a reservation. As far as she was concerned, they weren't accepting anyone for a day or so out of respect for the investigation. The last thing the sheriff needed was new people who could potentially mess up the crime scene.

A low voice responded to Linc's question, but Brigid couldn't make out what was said.

"Don't worry, we're not taking on any more guests at the moment," Brigid reassured Amanda. She could see that Amanda was worried a stranger might come in through the door, and Brigid couldn't blame her. She was in an extremely vulnerable state, and she didn't need anything else added to her plate at this point.

Brigid looked up in surprise as the door opened. *What is Linc doing?* she wondered. *Surely he's not bringing a drop-in guest inside?* As the door opened, he gave her an apologetic look.

"There's someone here who says he's Amanda's father," he said, sounding a little unsure.

"It can't be," Amanda said softly. "I just got off the phone with him."

Linc pushed the door open and as the older man stepped inside, Amanda's face lit up. She slid out from under Jett and rushed over to him with open arms. "Daddy," she said happily. "How are you already here?"

Brigid was wondering the exact same thing. She took in the older man who still seemed to be in fairly good shape for his age. He looked to be about ten years older than Brigid, maybe a little more.

"I'm sorry, honey, I should have told you," he said gently. Jett slipped off the couch and stood in front of Brigid. "I followed you and Brett here because I was afraid things might not go well."

"You must be psychic or something because things are definitely not going well," Amanda said as she began to cry again.

"Don't you worry, sweet pea. I'm here," he said as he pulled her into his arms again, and she began to cry even harder. It was as if she'd been holding it all in, but now that her father was here, everything had changed, and the dam that had held back her tears had burst.

"I'll get you a room here," Brigid said as she stood up and headed towards the desk.

"That's not necessary," he said. "I'm staying at the other B & B in town."

Brigid stopped in her tracks and turned. "Oh, I see. Well then, let me give you two a little privacy. I'll step outside." Her mind was spinning at this newest revelation, and she felt like she needed a little fresh air so she could think.

"Oh, where are my manners?" Amanda said as she wiped her eyes. "Dad, this is Brigid Olsen. She owns this B & B with her husband Linc. He's the one you met outside. They're wonderful people and have been taking good care of me. Brigid, this is my dad, Ed Hawthorne. Oh! And that's Jett," she said as she pointed to the dog that had hopped off the couch and was standing near Brigid.

"Nice to meet you, Brigid," he said with a nod. "That's a fine-looking dog you have there."

"Thank you," Brigid said as she moved towards the door. Jett stayed next to her, pausing to sniff Ed's boots.

"Like I said, I'll just be outside." She put her hand on the knob and realized that Jett hadn't moved. A low growl came from deep within him.

"Jett!" Brigid said surprised. "Come." Jett hesitated, looking from the man to Amanda, but then he followed Brigid. "I'm so sorry, he's usually friendly."

"Maybe he smells something he doesn't like on your boots," Amanda suggested. "He's been a sweetheart to me." She looked down at Jett confused, and Brigid had to admit that she felt the same way. Why would Jett react that way?

"Maybe," Ed said, eyeing the dog. "You just never know."

"Again, sorry," Brigid said as she ushered Jett out onto the porch.

Once outside, she hurried over to Linc. "That's odd," she said quietly.

"What?" Linc said.

"They live over three hours away and her dad just happened to be in town because he was worried about his daughter," Brigid said. "That seems fishy to me."

"You might want to call the sheriff," Linc suggested. "It's definitely worth looking into."

"Yeah, I think you're right," Brigid nodded. She pulled out her phone to find the sheriff's contact and then pressed the call button.

CHAPTER SEVENTEEN

"Sheriff? I think we have a new development here," Brigid said as Sheriff Davis answered.

"I'm all ears, Brigid. What ya' got?" he asked as she walked farther away from the B & B. Linc followed, so he could listen to her side of the conversation.

"Shortly after you left, Amanda made a phone call to her father to let him know about Brett. She told me that he promised to be on his way and that he lived three hours away. But less than fifteen minutes later he was walking through the door."

Brigid could feel something deep in her bones saying that this was important, that it was no coincidence.

"Really," Sheriff Davis said. "And she didn't know anythin'?"

"No," Brigid said. "She seemed genuinely surprised when he showed up. He said he was worried that she and Brett might have some trouble this weekend, and he wanted to be close, just in case."

"I'm thinkin' it seems a little too convenient," Sheriff Davis commented.

"I agree," Brigid said. "And Jett growled at him. I've never known

Jett to growl at anyone he just met. Something isn't right about all of this."

"Did he mention where he was stayin'?" Sheriff Davis asked.

"He just said the other B & B in town, so I assume it's Rich's place. I think we may want to do a little digging."

"Agreed," Sheriff Davis said. "I'm still workin' with Deputy Keegan on this footprint and shell casin'. Can ya' come to the sheriff's department in say… twenty minutes and then you and me can go talk to Rich?"

"Definitely," Brigid said. "In the meantime, I'll go in and talk to Amanda and her dad to see if I can get any information from them. Like how long he's been here and what he was doing last night around 9:00 p.m."

"Excellent idea," Sheriff Davis said. "See you then." Brigid hung up her phone and slid it into her pocket.

"What did he say?" Linc asked.

"Corey thinks we should look into her dad," Brigid said. "He agrees that something about this doesn't sit right."

"He'd certainly have a motive for wanting something to happen to Brett," Linc said. He and Brigid were standing side by side, looking back at the house with apprehension. "I mean, imagine if it were Holly being treated the way we saw him treating Amanda."

"I know," Brigid sighed. "I hate to admit it, but it all seems to fit together nicely. As long as he has a weapon and the footprints match."

"How are you going to find that out?" Linc asked.

"As for the shoes, I'll have to wait and see what they find from the plaster impression they made of the print. As you know, there are ways to tell what kind of a gun the murder weapon was. I don't know how we'd find out if he was behind the house last night. How could he have known that Brett would be out there?" Brigid still felt as though there were too many questions and not enough answers.

"Maybe we should go visit with them and see if we can work more information out of them," he suggested. "It's worth a shot."

Brigid nodded. "Let's go talk to them."

As they returned to the B & B and prepared to go inside, Jett decided to stay outside. "Jett, you sure you don't want to come in, buddy?" Linc asked as he held the door open for the dog. The big, hairy dog looked up and seemed to say, 'I'm not moving,' before he laid down on the porch. "Okay then," Linc said as he shut the door behind him.

"So, you've been in town over at the Cottonwood Springs B & B?" Brigid asked as they rejoined Amanda and Ed.

"I have," he said with a smile. "It's a nice place. Different from yours, but still good for an older gentleman like myself."

"Rich Jennings, the man who runs it, is a good friend of ours," Brigid said as she took a seat. "He's actually the one who suggested we open a B & B of our own."

"That's wonderful," Ed said, sounding genuine. "I want to thank you for taking such good care of my little Amanda here. This has been tough on her, but I know she'll come out of this situation just fine. She's a strong one. Always has been." He looked over at his daughter fondly as she blushed.

"Oh, Dad," she said, slightly embarrassed. "I don't know about all of that."

"I do," he said proudly. "You always were a tough cookie." He turned to Brigid and Linc, "Not like she was a fighter. No. She was just really good at dealing with tough situations and not letting them drag her down. She's a glass half-full kind of girl. Always has been."

"That's a good way to look at things," Linc said. He was leaning on the chair that Brigid was sitting in. "Never hurts to try to find some good in dark times. Sometimes when things get tough that's how we keep our chin above water."

"Exactly," Ed said happily. "She said you two offered to let her stay here a few extra days free of charge. That's such a kind gesture, and I really appreciate it. You didn't have to offer to do that."

"Not a problem at all," Brigid said. "I wouldn't want my daughter having to worry about everything that Amanda's going to have to and then deal with finances on top of all that."

"I think we'll stick around for the day," Ed said. "Maybe take a little drive and chat. Then we'll see about going home tomorrow. What do you say?" he asked as he looked at his daughter.

"I think I'd like that." She turned to Brigid. "You're B & B is beautiful and you two have been nothing but nice to me, but I think I'm ready to put this place behind me. You don't think the sheriff will need me to stay here, do you?"

Brigid looked up at Linc and debated on what to say. "Not that I'm aware of, but I'm going to go meet with the sheriff soon, so I'll check with him." She focused her attention on Ed. "You see, I actually work with the sheriff's department to help them solve cases."

Ed seemed surprised at that. "Oh really? Well that's interesting. How did you manage that?"

"It's a long story," Brigid said with a chuckle. "But let's just say I seem to have a knack for finding clues and following leads. Since I'm not officially an officer, I'm not bogged down by the protocol the other officers have to follow, so I intend to focus on finding whoever committed the murder of your son-in-law. I promise you both, I won't rest until I've found out who did this."

115

"I really appreciate that," Amanda said softly. "Brett may have had his flaws, but he didn't deserve that."

"Well, it's already getting on in the day," Ed said. "I think we'll go take that drive now. But first, we'll stop by the B & B where I'm staying. I was in such a hurry to get over here that I didn't even grab my wallet." He laughed good naturedly as he stood up. "It's been a pleasure chatting with you two," he said, extending his hand to both Linc and Brigid.

"Same, but I wish we'd met under better circumstances," Linc said.

"Me, too," Ed said soberly.

"Let me run a brush through my hair, and I'll be right there," Amanda said. She took off for her room as Ed nodded and stepped outside. After a few moments, Amanda reappeared and gave them a little wave before rushing out the front door.

Brigid and Linc both watched from the front window as they climbed into Ed's Malibu and drove away.

"Do you think we should have tried to make them stay?" Linc asked.

"No," Brigid said, shaking her head. "We don't know anything for sure. Besides, if Ed did kill Brett, we don't want to tip him off. We have to move very carefully, otherwise, he might run. We need him to be confident, that way he won't be as concerned with covering his tracks."

Linc nodded. "Makes sense. I guess if he is the killer, maybe it's good for he and his daughter to have a nice day. She'll need it."

"I was thinking the same thing," Brigid said as her phone began to ring. Pulling it out, she saw that it was her sister. "It's Fiona," she said to Linc before answering.

"Why have I not gotten a call from my sister telling me about a MURDER THAT HAPPENED IN HER BACKYARD?" Fiona shrieked into the phone.

"Hello to you, too," Brigid said as she pulled the phone away from her ear. "I haven't had a chance to do much of anything," she explained. "It's nothing personal."

"Please tell me that Sheriff Davis already has the killer apprehended and everything is all good," Fiona sighed. "Please tell me that."

"Well..." Brigid paused. "Not exactly, but he's working on it."

"Holly just told me. Do I need to be worried about your safety?" Fiona asked.

"Definitely not," Brigid said confidently. "You know I've had a lot of law enforcement training. I can handle myself."

"What happened?" Fiona asked.

Brigid tried her best to explain the situation. She reminded Fiona about the couple she'd spoken about when she visited her and told her what had happened since then. She didn't tell Fiona about her suspicions concerning Amanda's father, but she told her everything else.

"Wow," was all Fiona could muster. After a brief silence, she said, "So what's next?"

"Right now I need to go see the sheriff and see what they've learned from the evidence they collected. I have a feeling I have a full day ahead of me," Brigid sighed.

"Sounds like it. I think I'll invite Holly over for pizza tonight if that's okay with you. She seemed a little stressed over everything, so I thought I'd let her come over and veg out with me. Brandon's going to be working late, and you know how well she gets along with

Aiden."

"Sure, that would be great. Just let her know I'm working to get to the bottom of it, and she doesn't have anything to worry about," Brigid said.

"Will do," Fiona said before she hung up. Brigid told Linc how Holly would most likely be eating dinner with Fiona.

"Then I guess you better get going," he sighed. "I'll stick around here and tell you if I see anything odd. You never know, the murderer might return to try to cover their tracks."

"If you see someone, do not go out there," Brigid insisted. "Call Sheriff Davis immediately."

"Relax, I know the drill," he said with a smirk. "You know, you aren't the only one with skills. Remember, I'm the one who first taught you how to use a gun." He gave her a playful wink, and she couldn't help but smile.

"Oh, I remember," she said flirting. "Maybe I'll help get this person behind bars and you and me can have a little date night."

"Hmmm, that would be nice," Linc said with a grin. "I could always make your favorite for dinner. I'm thinking lamb chops with bacon green beans, and for dessert, Amaretto cake."

"You really know how to make a girl look forward to dinner," she said. Leaning forward she gave him a long, passionate kiss. "That's a preview for later."

"Can't wait," he said. "But you better take off for the sheriff's department before he thinks you're not coming and leaves without you."

"You have a point," she said as she stepped back. "I love you, and I'll let you know what we find."

"I love you too," Linc said. "Now get out there and help Corey catch the bad guys." He gave her bottom a playful swat as she turned and headed for the door.

CHAPTER EIGHTEEN

Brigid pulled up in front of the sheriff's department and was glad to see that not only Sheriff Davis's patrol truck, but also Deputy Keegan's patrol car, were still parked nearby.

Good, she thought. *They haven't decided to go follow up on a lead or something they may have found.* She got out of her car and hurried toward the building.

As she entered, the cooler air of the building greeted her. She didn't have to come into the sheriff's station all that often, but when she did, she was always greeted with smiling faces.

"We're back here," Sheriff Davis called out as he poked his head out of one of the conference rooms. Brigid rounded the counter that divided the desks from the public waiting area and headed for the grey door.

"Hey, guys," she said as she entered. "How are things on your end?"

"Not bad," Sheriff Davis said with a single nod. "Told Deputy Keegan everythin' ya' told me, so she's up to speed."

"Good," Brigid said. "You should also know that the father, Ed Hawthorne, is encouraging his daughter to go home tomorrow. If we're going to look into him, we need to move quickly."

"No problem. We need to go speak with Rich and see what he's got to say about his guest. I'd like to know what he thinks of him." Sheriff Davis turned to Deputy Keegan, "Wanna' tell Brigid what ya' found?"

"Sure," she said with a nod. "The murder weapon looks to be a handgun of some sort. Nothing too fancy. The boot print was what held my interest for the most part," she said.

"I'm surprised you found any footprints out there," Brigid interrupted. "It hasn't rained for a while."

"True," Keegan said. "But there was a little dip in the ground that was still a bit muddy. That's where I got this great print. After I did a little research on it, I found out that only one brand has this particular sole pattern and the foot is fairly large. Size thirteen."

Brigid recalled the boots Amanda's father was wearing. "Any idea what these boots look like?"

"I can't say for sure," Keegan said, shaking her head. "But they're definitely a brand called Outlanders. Their unique soles look like mountain ranges, see," she said as she lifted up a photo she'd made of the footprint and handed it to Brigid.

"That is different," Brigid said. "So what we're looking for is someone with a handgun and these unique boots," she summarized.

"Any idea what brand of boots this dad wears?" Sheriff Davis asked.

"Sorry, I didn't look at them that closely," Brigid said, shaking her head.

"You know, you could always look around at Rich's for similar boot prints," Deputy Keegan suggested. "Maybe you'll get lucky?"

"Worth a shot," Sheriff Davis said. "Keep workin' with the computer and see if ya' can find out any more about the gun. We'll go see if Rich can tell us if his guest was there last night or not. If he was tucked in tight, then we're barkin' up the wrong tree."

"Will do," Deputy Keegan said. "Good luck."

Brigid followed Sheriff Davis out of the conference room. "What are we going to do if it doesn't look like her dad did it?"

"Jes' keep searchin'," he said simply. "After all, whoever did it had to get there somewhere. If they..." He stopped in mid-sentence and turned towards Brigid. "Wait, why didn't I think of that before?"

"What?" Brigid asked. "What am I missing?"

"The woods," he said. "They're far enough in that they're right on the border of yer' property. The rest is mostly wooded area. Some people like to have trail cams up to watch fer trespassers."

"Trail cams?" Brigid asked, confused. "Aren't those the cameras hunters use to find deer?"

"That they do," he said, nodding. "But people use 'em fer security purposes, too. Maybe whoever owns the land has somethin' like that out there. Ya' know who owns the land?"

Brigid shook her head. "Not for sure."

"That's okay," he said. "We gotta' database. I'll tell Keegan to check on it. Wait right here." He dashed back into the conference room before reappearing a moment later. "Okay, let's go."

They left the sheriff's department and climbed into his truck. "Know this is gonna' sound crazy, but I hope it's not her father," he said after they shut their doors.

"I hear you," Brigid said as she fastened her seat belt. "After all, if it was him, he probably did it to protect Amanda."

"Can't imagine bein' in that position," the sheriff mused as he began to drive. "You said the victim was a real piece of work. Knowin' yer' little girl was being mistreated….," he let his sentence trail off. "Course that don't give him the right to take matters into his own hands, but still."

"I agree," Brigid said. "Her mother passed away a while back. I'm sure he's just trying to take care of his little girl."

"Exactly, but it's gonn'a be a little hard to do that if he's behind bars," Sheriff Davis pointed out.

"Fair point," Brigid nodded. "For her sake and his, I hope it wasn't him."

Soon they were pulling up outside of the other B & B in town that was run by the former sheriff, Rich Jennings. There were no other vehicles there besides Rich's old Ford truck, so they knew that, at least for now, Ed Hawthorne wasn't around.

"Let's go see what Rich has got to say," Sheriff Davis said as he opened his door.

"Well land's sakes, look who we have here," Rich said as he stepped outside. "How are you two doing on this beautiful day?"

"Been better," Sheriff Davis said. "Can we speak to ya' fer a bit?"

"Sure. Come on in and sit a spell," Rich said as he waved them inside. He led them over to a seating area and paused. "Can I get you two anything? Coffee? Tea?"

"We're good, thanks," Brigid said. "We just have a few questions."

"Okay," Rich said as he took a seat. "Well, what can I do ya' for?"

"Need to ask ya' 'bout your guest, Ed Hawthorne," Sheriff Davis said, getting straight to the point.

"Nice gentleman, kinda quiet, and keeps to himself. Why are you asking about him?" Rich asked, squinting.

"We're wondering if he was here last night around 9:00," Brigid said.

"Nine, you say?" Rich repeated as he stroked his chin. "No, I don't believe he was, but he was at breakfast this morning. Why do you ask?"

"There was a murder last night behind Brigid's B & B, and Ed's son-in-law was the victim. We've placed the time of death around 9:00 p.m."

"No, he was definitely gone around that time. I'd say he left sometime around dusk. But then, he has every night he's been here. I know because he leaves before the early news," Rich said.

"Noticed anythin' odd about him?" Sheriff Davis asked.

"Well, I noticed he carries," Rich began. "Although that's not a crime."

"Any idea what he has?" Brigid asked.

"I'm not sure. I'd say something small from the telltale bulge under his jacket," Rich admitted. "But we had a conversation one morning about his years in the service. I just assumed that he'd been through some stuff and felt better having something on him. You know how some people are."

Sheriff Davis nodded. "Anythin' else? Carryin' a gun ain't exactly damnin' evidence."

"Actually, there is something, now that you mention it. He came back from being gone for a while and went to his room. When he came back out, he asked where the trash cans were. I told him they were behind the house. He had a plastic bag tied off with something in it, but I just figured it was trash. He tossed it in the can and left again." Rich shrugged.

"Would you mind if we took a look at what he threw away?" Brigid asked.

"It shouldn't be a problem," Rich shrugged. "After all, trash is trash. And if it helps, I have cameras out back that are motion-activated. I got them when I had raccoons getting into them a while back. I was beginning to wonder if someone was messing with me, so I got the cameras to be sure."

"Might be helpful, dependin' on what's in the bag," Sheriff Davis said as he stood up. He turned to Brigid, "I'll go take a quick look. Stay here if ya' want."

Brigid nodded and turned back to Rich as the sheriff went outside. "How's business?" she asked, making conversation.

"Not too bad. I only have the one guest at the moment, but by next weekend I should be almost full. How about you?"

"Slowly picking up," Brigid said with a smile. "I'd say we're doing pretty good, considering."

"Hope this situation you've found yourself in doesn't put a damper on things," Rich sighed. "That'd be a shame. But I bet it will blow over," he said confidently.

Sheriff Davis returned after a few moments, holding a bag with gloved hands. "He threw away boots. And get this, they're size thirteen and they got the same tread."

"Rich, I think we may need that footage," Brigid said carefully.

"Not a problem. Let me go put it on one of those stick things for you," he said as he stood and hurried off.

"This don't look very good for Ed Hawthorne," Sheriff Davis said. "And I think it gives me enough probable cause to get a search warrant."

"I think you're right," Brigid agreed.

CHAPTER NINETEEN

"We've got the warrant," Sheriff Davis said as he returned to the truck. He and Brigid had left Rich's and headed straight to the judge to talk to him about searching Ed Hawthorne's room at the B & B.

"Did you really have to have a warrant for his room?" Brigid asked. "I mean after all, it's Rich's house."

"It's a bit of a grey area," Sheriff Davis admitted. "Rather have one and do everythin' by the book, although I ain't feelin' the greatest about this."

"No, I don't either," Brigid agreed. "But he also doesn't have the right to take the law into his own hands."

"Yeah, I know," Sheriff Davis said with a sigh. "Come on, let's go." He pulled away and they began the trip back to Rich's when Brigid's phone began to ring.

"Hello?" she answered.

"Brigid, it's Deputy Keegan. I figured the sheriff might be busy, so I just called you. I'm sending an image I got from one of the nearby landowners of a man walking into the treeline wearing camo. I did my best to get you a clear face picture," she said. Brigid pulled the phone away and looked through her email.

"I got it," Brigid said as she opened it. "I'm looking at it now." As she zoomed in on the man's face, she realized she recognized him. "That's Ed Hawthorne, the father-in-law," Brigid said.

"Camera's got him walking into the trees around the right time for him to be our killer," Deputy Keegan said.

"Thank you," Brigid said as she hung up. She turned to Sheriff Davis, "I really didn't want it to be him."

"I didn't either," he admitted. "But now we got enough evidence to place him under arrest. Anythin' else we find will just be icin' on the cake."

When they pulled up at Rich's B & B, they hurried inside. Sheriff Davis showed the warrant to Rich who led them straight to Ed's room and opened it for them. The room was still fairly clean. He'd made his own bed, and all of his things were neatly folded in the dresser.

Sheriff Davis pulled open a dresser drawer and saw a handgun laying on top of camouflage clothing. "Looks like we got the weapon," he said.

The sound of a car pulling up outside caused Brigid to look out the window. "Ed's back with Amanda," she said.

"I've seen enough," Sheriff Davis said sounding almost sad. "Better go do what needs to be done." They turned and left the room, heading for the entry. As they descended the stairs, Amanda and Ed walked through the door.

"Brigid, what are you doing here?" Amanda asked.

"I know why they're here," Ed said solemnly. "They're here to arrest me."

"But why?" Amanda asked, clearly shocked.

"Ed Hawthorne, you are under arrest for the murder of Brett Stephenson," Sheriff Davis said as he approached the man. He began reading him his Miranda rights as he placed handcuffs on him. Ed didn't move and simply accepted what was happening.

"Daddy, why?" Amanda asked. Ed looked over at Brigid and then at the sheriff.

"I think we can let you two talk for a few minutes before we take him in," Brigid said as she glanced at Sheriff Davis.

"You know how I felt about the way Brett treated you," Ed began. "I promised your mother I'd protect you after she was gone, and I took that promise to heart. I couldn't stand the way he was with you. He was cruel and hateful, not how a husband should be.

"So when you called to tell me you were coming here, I couldn't just let you go. I was afraid that something might happen to you, and I'd be too far away to help. I came here and drove around, finding out where you were staying and everything. When you called me and told me about the bruises he left on your arm, I knew what I had to do."

"Wait, bruises?" Brigid asked.

Amanda sighed and looked down. She lifted her sleeve first to show her upper arm covered in purple marks. They were clearly fingerprints where someone had wrapped their hand around her and squeezed.

"He was really mad when he thought there was something going on with Eric," she said softly. She lowered her sleeve and then pulled up the hem of her shirt to show a few more bruises that were purple. But Brigid noticed something else.

"What about those yellow ones?" she asked gently.

"Those were from another time," Amanda said simply.

"That's why I was in the woods that night," Ed admitted. "She told me he'd been hurting her recently, and I'd had enough. I didn't think about killing him."

"Why did ya' have the gun?" Sheriff Davis asked.

"I always carry it. You can ask anyone back home. It's as much a part of me as anything else I wear. I'd been trying to watch to make sure he didn't hurt her. It was just coincidence that they walked back to the woods. I heard the whole exchange of her telling him he needed to straighten up or she was gone.

"But after she'd left, he stayed and was talking to himself. I stuck around to hear what he had to say, and I heard him planning to kill her. I was afraid for her life considering what he'd already done to her. I didn't think I could let him go back into that house with her. Before I knew what I was doing, I'd pulled out my gun and shot him."

Sheriff Davis pulled out his notepad and began writing. "Need ya' both to come down to the station with me," he said. He tore out the piece of paper he'd written something on and handed it to Amanda.

"I want ya' to call this guy today and tell him what's happened. Make sure ya' tell him I tol' ya' to call. He's an old friend and in my opinion, he's the best criminal defense lawyer in Colorado. He can help yer' dad with his case."

"I don't have a lot of money," she began.

"That's why I want ya' to tell him I sent ya. He owes me," Sheriff Davis smirked. "I don't mind callin' in one of my favors fer ya'." He leaned towards his radio and called for Deputy Keegan to meet him to transport.

Brigid smiled as she looked at her friend. She'd always known that Sheriff Davis had a big heart, but now she had proof. To help people he didn't even know by letting them call in a favor was no small thing. She reached out and placed her hand on his forearm and smiled. He looked up in surprise and smiled back.

*****

"Don't worry, I know it's a little scary to have your dad in jail but he'll be taken care of here," Brigid assured Amanda as she sat in the conference room at the sheriff's station.

"I know, and I appreciate everything you and the sheriff have done," she said. "I just wish none of this would have happened. I feel like it's all my fault." A tear slid down her face, and she brushed it away angrily.

"How in the world could it be your fault?" Brigid asked gently.

"If I never would have fallen in love with Brett, or if I'd left him when my mom told me to," she sniffed, "Brett wouldn't be dead, and Dad wouldn't be in jail."

Brigid understood what was going on here all too well. "Amanda, listen to me," she began. "You did what you thought was right. You stayed with your husband because you believed that was what you should do. I'm sure you never thought it would ever turn out this way, did you?"

Amanda shook her head. "Which is why it's not your fault," Brigid continued. "If you'd known, you would have done things differently, but there's no sense to beat yourself up over things you didn't know. All you can do is move forward, and besides, you don't know what may have happened to you if your father hadn't made that hard choice. What if it had been you I found instead of Brett?"

"That's a terrifying thought," Amanda admitted.

"And one I'm sure will be brought up in court. Your father was afraid for your life. I can't believe a jury will hear that and not feel compassion for you and your father. Don't be afraid to tell your story. Maybe you can help save someone else."

Brigid could tell that Amanda hadn't considered that, and she seemed to hold herself up a little straighter. A knock on the door interrupted them.

"Come on in," Brigid said.

Deputy Keegan stepped through the door and gave them both a small smile. "Hello, ladies. I'm here to take the photos Sheriff Davis requested."

Amanda looked over at Brigid who nodded. "It's okay. I know it's not exactly fun, but we need to document the injuries that Brett gave you. This will help your father's case."

Amanda nodded and stood up from her chair. "Where do you want me?"

Deputy Keegan looked around the room and pointed to a nearby corner. "How about right there?" she said. Amanda nodded and went over to where the deputy had pointed. When she looked around nervously, Brigid reached for the door and locked it.

"It's just the two of us and Deputy Keegan is my friend. You're safe, I promise."

Amanda took a deep breath and tugged her shirt over her head. The dark purple marks on her ribs and upper arms seemed so much darker in the florescent lights, and made Brigid suck in her breath. "He only hurt you where he knew no one would be able to see the bruises," she said.

Amanda nodded. "He didn't use to but recently…," she stopped as she started to cry.

"It's okay, honey," Deputy Keegan said. "You're not the only one who's been on the other side of this camera. I have too."

Both Brigid and Amanda were surprised. "Really?" Amanda asked as she turned and lifted her arm, letting Deputy Keegan take a picture.

"I have. I had an abusive boyfriend right out of high school. Actually, he's part of the reason I joined the academy. I wanted to be there for other women to see that there's something on the other side of all of this." She gave Amanda a sympathetic smile and then said. "Is that all of them?"

Amanda looked nervous. "Not really."

"Wherever they are, we need to document them so the court can see," Deputy Keegan reminded her.

Amanda nodded. "Can I put my shirt back on first?"

"Absolutely," Deputy Keegan said.

Amanda tugged her shirt on and then began to unzip her pants. "This one's older, but it's still there." As she lowered her jeans, she showed them a large bruise on her side. It was obvious that it had faded some, but there were still vivid purples and blues that looked painful. "He pushed me into the kitchen counter," she explained.

"Thank you," Deputy Keegan said as they finished.

"I should be thanking you," Amanda said.

"No, thank you for speaking up," Deputy Keegan said. "It's important that women like you and me show others that we don't have to hide. That there are other people out there who understand and are willing to listen. We won't judge those women going through these things. We won't ask them why they're wearing something or what they did to deserve this, because we know and understand that those questions hurt. They may not mean anything by asking them, but that doesn't mean that they don't hurt all the same."

"You ladies are inspiring," Brigid finally said. She'd been so in awe of the strength they'd both shown that she was having a hard time speaking. "I'm proud to say I know you both."

EPILOGUE

"Oh, look," Brigid said from the office at the B & B. "We got an email from Amanda."

It had been a while since Brigid had heard from her and her father, so it was a welcome surprise.

Lucky came running around the corner as Holly appeared at the door. "What's it say?" she asked as she leaned on the door.

"She says she's doing better. It's taken some time to get used to living alone, but she's liking it. She's hopeful her dad is going to get a reduced sentence."

"That would be awesome," Holly interjected.

Brigid picked up Lucky and began scratching his belly as she scanned the email for more. "She also says she's still talking to Eric. I guess he found her on social media and said he'd like to keep in touch. Is that not the greatest thing ever?" Brigid gasped.

"Aww!" Holly cried. "That's so cute!"

"Why thank you," Linc said as he came in the back door. "I'll take that as a compliment." He gave them both a cheesy grin and they laughed.

"Not you, you dork," Holly said, playfully slapping him. "Eric reached out to Amanda on social media."

"So?" Linc asked.

"He's respecting that she needs space, but he still likes her enough to want to stay in touch. Like he's there for her," Holly said.

"That's cute," Linc said with a smile. "Maybe we can start advertising that romance starts at the New Dawn B & B?"

"I think the fact that a man lost his life in the process kind of negates the whole thing," Brigid pointed out.

"Yeah, I guess you're right," he sighed.

"She says she's definitely not ready for dating or anything like that, but it's nice to have someone to talk to, which I can understand. Eric was here, so he knows what happened, at least to a certain degree," Brigid pointed out.

"Very true," Holly nodded.

"It's nice that she reached out," Linc said as he grabbed a glass of lemonade. "Have the Petersons checked in yet?"

Brigid looked at the time. "Not yet, but they should be here any minute. I should probably go out to the living room and wait for them." She set Lucky back down on the floor and stood up.

"I'll wait with you," Holly offered.

"Don't leave me out," Linc said as he hurried to join them.

"I'm still so excited for Fiona," Holly said as they all took a seat in the living room.

"I know," Brigid agreed. "I tried to tell her there was no way they'd turn her down. And I think the fact that they approved her for both seasons just based on her designs really shows she has what it takes."

"Maybe you should throw a party for her?" Linc suggested. "Like a surprise one to celebrate her success?"

"That's a great idea!" Holly said eagerly. "Can I do it?"

Brigid and Linc looked over at her in surprise. "Sure, if you want," Brigid said. "If you need any help, just let me know."

"Awesome," Holly said with a grin. "This is going to be fun."

"Looks like the Petersons are here," Linc said as a car slowed to pull into the small gravel parking lot.

"Well, back to business as usual at the New Dawn B & B," Holly sighed.

"You got that right," Linc said with a grin. He stood up and opened the door for the couple as they approached the front door. "Hello, and welcome to the New Dawn B & B," he said happily. "You must be the Petersons."

"We are," said the older gentleman. He was wearing a brown suit and a blue tie. "I'm Bernard and this is my wife, Dorothy." He patted her hand affectionately. She was wearing a white dress and a small straw hat with flowers. "We're celebrating our honeymoon."

"Congratulations!" Brigid said as she stood up. She introduced herself to them and had them check in.

Linc showed them to their room as Holly stood up and walked over to the desk. "Sounds like it's time for another pin in the map," she said with a grin. Pulling one out of the drawer, she went to the large corkboard on the map and then pulled out her phone. "Now to search for it so I can get it in the right spot."

"I think you've become a little obsessed with this map," Brigid chuckled as she joined her.

Holly shrugged. "It's fun. And I've noticed that guests think it's pretty cool too. They like to see where people are from."

"Whatever makes you happy," Brigid sighed. "I don't think I'd have the patience to keep that up."

"Give it time," Holly grinned. "I'll have you hooked on it too. I almost have Linc hooked."

"Okay, kiddo," Linc said as he reappeared. "You have your phone out yet?"

"Told you," Holly said with a grin directed at Brigid. "Sure do," she said louder to him. "I was just about to place the pin."

"This was a great idea," Linc said happily. "I love watching the little pins bring color to the map." He finally noticed that Brigid was simply staring at him. "What?" he asked innocently.

"You two," she said, shaking her head. "I swear."

Linc looked at Holly. "What's her deal?" he asked as he hitched his thumb at her.

"I guess she's just not a cool kid," Holly teased as she turned toward the map. She and Linc began to look for just the right spot and then she pushed in the pin.

Brigid left the two of them to marvel at the map. She stepped out onto the front porch and breathed in the fresh air. As the sun set in the distance, she could almost sense the cooler temperatures coming. School was about to start and then before she knew it, winter would be here. She thought about how the B & B would look with Christmas lights and a beautiful blanket of snow on everything.

Jett appeared beside her and bumped her hand with his nose. She smiled as she looked down at him and stroked the fur on the top of his head. "This is it, Jett," she said feeling content. "This is the good life."

RECIPES

GARLIC & BACON GREEN BEANS

Ingredients:
½ lb. fresh green beans, rinsed, ends snapped off & broken into 1-1 ½ inch pieces
¼ tsp. salt
1 tbsp. olive oil
1 tbsp. butter
6 garlic cloves, rough chopped
4 bacon strips, fried & drained of fat
¼ cup sliced almonds, lightly toasted in small dry skillet

Directions:
Place beans in a medium size saucepan, cover with water (water should be about 1" above the beans). Add salt and bring to a boil over medium heat. Boil for 5 minutes, turn off heat and drain beans. Fry the bacon in a large skillet until crisp, remove and drain grease from pan. While still warm, cut the bacon strips with kitchen scissors into large pieces, about 1 – 1 ½ inches long and set aside.

Heat the olive oil and butter in the same large skillet (leaving any brown residue left from frying the bacon). Add chopped garlic and cook over medium heat for 1-2 minutes until just soft, stirring constantly. Add chopped cooked bacon, toasted almonds, beans, and sauté on medium high heat for 2 minutes, stirring to combine all ingredients. Remove from heat and serve. Enjoy!

NOTE: I've also used broccoli instead of green beans and it was every bit as good.

CHARLOTTE'S AMARETTO CAKE W/WHITE SYRUP GLAZE

Ingredients:
Cake:
1 pkg. yellow cake mix
4 eggs
½ cup canola oil
½ cup water
½ cup Amaretto
¼ cup crushed almonds
Cooking spray

White Syrup:
½ cup unsalted butter
1 cup sugar
¼ cup water
1/8 tsp. almond extract
½ cup Amaretto
¼ cup crushed almonds

Directions:
Cake:
Preheat oven to 350 degrees. Mix the cake ingredients, except the ground almonds, in a medium-size mixing bowl until well combined. Spray cooking spray on bottom & sides of Bundt pan, add ground almonds evenly to the bottom of the pan, and then pour the cake batter into the pan. Bake for 45-50 minutes, testing for doneness with a slender wooden probe. Remove cake from oven & cool in the pan for 20 minutes on a wire rack. When cooled, remove cake from Bundt pan and place on a serving plate.

White Syrup Glaze:

While the cake is cooling, combine butter, sugar, & water in a medium-size saucepan and bring to a boil over medium-high heat. Remove from heat, allow to cool slightly so it is just warm, then add the Amaretto and almond extract, stirring to combine well.

After the cake has been removed from the Bundt pan and placed on a serving plate, using a wooden dowel approx. ¼" in diameter, poke holes in the entire top of the cake. The holes should be about 2" from each other and penetrate the cake to a depth of about ½ the height of the cake.

NOTE: If you don't have a wooden dowel, try using a fork or other kitchen tool, or even a pencil, to make the holes. Wiggle the wooden dowel to enlarge the holes slightly so the warm syrup will easily flow into each hole. Use a teaspoon to fill the holes with the syrup.

Gently pour ½ of the syrup on top of the cake, so most of it soaks down into the holes. Then slowly pour the remaining half of the syrup on the top inner and outer edge of the cake so it runs evenly down the sides of the cake. While the syrup is still warm and sticky, sprinkle ground almonds evenly on top of the cake. Serve at room temperature and enjoy!

NOTE: It's hard to find crushed almonds, so place a handful of almonds in a plastic bag and crush, using a meat mallet or a hammer. Crush until the consistency is fine.

CLASSIC RAISIN SAUCE FOR BAKED HAM

Ingredients:
½ cup brown sugar
2 tbsp. corn starch
1 tsp. dry mustard
1 tbsp. white vinegar
1 cup raisins

¼ tsp. lemon zest, finely grated
2 tbsp. lemon juice
1 ½ cups water

Directions:
Combine brown sugar, cornstarch and dry mustard in a saucepan. Place the pan over medium heat and gradually add the vinegar, raisins, lemon zest, and lemon juice, stirring constantly. Add the water and continue to stir until thoroughly blended and thick. Serve in a gravy boat, ladling the sauce over the ham.

Variations: Add 1-2 tbsp. butter to the sauce as soon as it is removed from the heat. Replace ½ cup of water with orange juice or apple juice. Add ½ cup of diced apples and cook along with the raisins. For extra spice, add ½ tsp. of cinnamon, ¼ tsp. ground ginger & a dash of cloves. Or for a little kick, add 1 tsp. of dark rum.

STREUSEL COFFEE CAKE MUFFINS

Ingredients:
Streusel Topping:
½ cup brown sugar, firmly packed
½ cup all-purpose flour
½ tsp. ground cinnamon
¼ unsalted butter, cut into bits

Muffins:
1 ½ cups all-purpose flour
1 tsp. baking powder
1/8 tsp. baking soda
1 cup granulated sugar
½ cup unsalted butter, room temperature & cut into small bits
2 large eggs
½ cup sour cream
1 tsp. vanilla extract

Directions:
Topping:
Put the brown sugar, flour, and cinnamon in a food processor and pulse to combine. Drop the butter on top and pulse until the mixture begins to form small, pebble-like nuggets.

Muffins:
Preheat the oven to 450 degrees. Line 12 muffin cups with paper liners or coat with nonstick cooking spray. In a food processor, combine the flour, baking powder, baking soda, and sugar. Pulse 3 times. Sprinkle the butter over the dry ingredients and pulse until the mixture is the size of small peas. Add the eggs, sour cream, and vanilla and process for 30 seconds. Scrape down the sides of the work bowl and pulse until the batter is blended.

Scoop ¼ cup of the batter into each muffin cup and top with 1 tbsp. of the streusel topping. Bake until golden brown and a skewer inserted into the center comes out clean, approximately 15-17 minutes. Serve and enjoy!

BRIOCHE FRENCH BREAD

Ingredients:
1 tsp. ground cinnamon
¼ tsp. ground nutmeg
2 tbsp. sugar
4 tbsp. butter
4 eggs
¼ cup milk
1/8 tsp. vanilla extract
8 slices challah, brioche, or white bread
½ cup maple syrup, warmed

Directions:
In a small bowl, combine cinnamon, nutmeg, and sugar and set aside briefly.
In a 10-inch or 12-inch skillet, melt butter over medium heat.

Whisk together cinnamon mixture, eggs, milk, and vanilla and pour into a shallow container such as a pie plate. Dip bread in egg mixture. Fry slices until golden brown, then flip to cook the other side. Serve with warm syrup and enjoy!

LEAVE A REVIEW

I'd really appreciate it you could take a few seconds and leave a review of Murder at the New Dawn B & B

Just go to the link below. Thank you so much, it means a lot to me ~ Dianne

http://getbook.at/MND

Paperbacks & Ebooks for FREE

Go to www.dianneharman.com/freepaperback.html and get your FREE copies of Dianne's books and favorite recipes immediately by signing up for her newsletter.

Once you've signed up for her newsletter you're eligible to win three paperbacks. One lucky winner is picked every week. Hurry before the offer ends!

ABOUT THE AUTHOR

Dianne lives in Huntington Beach, California, with her husband, Tom, a former California State Senator, and her boxer dog, Kelly. Her passions are cooking, reading, and dogs, so whenever she has a little free time, you can either find her in the kitchen, playing with Kelly in the back yard, or curled up with the latest book she's reading. Her award-winning books include:

Cedar Bay Cozy Mystery Series

Cedar Bay Cozy Mystery Series - Boxed Set

Liz Lucas Cozy Mystery Series

Liz Lucas Cozy Mystery Series - Boxed Set

High Desert Cozy Mystery Series

High Desert Cozy Mystery Series - Boxed Set

Northwest Cozy Mystery Series

Northwest Cozy Mystery Series - Boxed Set

Midwest Cozy Mystery Series

Midwest Cozy Mystery Series - Boxed Set

Jack Trout Cozy Mystery Series

Cottonwood Springs Cozy Mystery Series

Cottonwood Springs Mystery Series – Boxed Set

Midlife Journey Series

Midlife Journey Series – Boxed Set

The Holly Lewis Mystery Series

The Holly Lewis Mystery Series – Boxed Set

Red Zero Series

Black Dot Series

Coyote Series

Newsletter

If you would like to be notified of her latest releases please go to www.dianneharman.com and sign up for her newsletter.

Website: www.dianneharman.com,
Blog: www.dianneharman.com/blog
Email: dianne@dianneharman.com

PUBLISHING 1/10/20

LITTLE FEATHER

BOOK ONE OF

MIRANDA RILEY PI PARANORMAL COZY MYSTERIES

http://getbook.at/MLF

All it takes is one phone call to change your life.

Miranda Riley was a blackjack dealer in Las Vegas when she received a call from the police that her mother, Eve, was missing. She rushed home to Little Feather, Oklahoma, hoping to quickly find her mother so she could return to her life in the big city.

But once Miranda begins to search for her, she finds there is much more to Little Feather and her mother than she originally thought. First, the city is an oasis for supernatural creatures, and secondly, her mother was the Paranormal Investigator who kept them all in line.

As a P.I., it was her mother's job to make sure the paranormal creatures stayed out of view from humans and didn't commit any crimes. But now that she's gone that's changing.

Miranda finds herself caught up in a world she never knew existed. She needs to find her mother before paranormal things get out of hand in Little Feather, and two very attractive men are willing to help her.

Open your smartphone, point and shoot at the QR code below. You will be taken to Amazon where you can pre-order 'Little Feather'.

(Download the QR code app onto your smartphone from the iTunes or Google Play store in order to read the QR code below.)

Made in the USA
Coppell, TX
10 November 2022

86127516R00090